D1000591

BREAKING AWAY!

"You girls are always causing trouble . . ." Coach Carpenter began.

"We didn't do it!" Breezy cut him off, not even noticing that the game had not resumed and that both teams, and everyone in the stands, was watching them.

Coach Carpenter sputtered and opened his mouth. "You two have disrupted my team for the last time! You've been nothing but trouble since the season started. You're both benched!"

Breezy couldn't help herself. She started laughing.

"Did you hear me?!" the coach screamed, putting his face right up to Breezy's.

"We've been benched since we joined this stupid league!" Breezy yelled back. "You can't bench me anymore —I quit!"

"Me, too," Kim echoed.

MEET THE PINK PARROTS:

Amy (Breezy) Hawk
Twelve years old, and the Pink Parrots star pitcher, Breezy's every inch the tomboy—and she knows baseball inside and out.

Jasmine (Jazz) Jaffe
Thirteen years old and the Parrots rightfielder as well as Breezy's cousin, Jazz is boy-crazy and prone to giggle atttacks. She wants to be a model.

Kim Yardley
Twelve-and-a-half and an excellent shortstop, Kim is Breezy's best friend. Fun-loving and joke-cracking, Kim is friends with everyone.

Theresa (Terry) DiSunno
Thirteen years old and the Parrots catcher, Terry's not fast, but she *is* a slugger. When she stops being hostile, she's a whole lot of fun.

Crystal Joseph
Thirteen years old and the Parrots first baseman, Crystal is 5'7" tall and a ballerina. And she's learning how to play baseball from a book!

Rose Anne (Ro) DiMona
The spirited owner of the Pink Parrots Beauty Salon, Ro is the team's sponsor and coach. Her clothes are wild and her training techniques are weird, but she's determined to make the Parrots the best team in the Eastern Maryland Baseball League.

THE PINK PARROTS

THE GIRLS STRIKE BACK
The Making of the Pink Parrots

Created by Lucy Ellis

By Kathilyn Solomon Proboz
with Leah Jerome

41052

A *SPORTS ILLUSTRATED FOR KIDS* BOOK

Created by Lucy Ellis
Written by Kathilyn Solomon Proboz
with Leah Jerome
Cover art by Jeff Mangiat
Interior line art by Jane Davila
Produced by Angel Entertainment, Inc.

SPORTS ILLUSTRATED FOR KIDS Books is a joint imprint of Little, Brown and Company and Warner Juvenile Books.

Printed in the United States of America

First Printing: September 1990
10 9 8 7 6 5 4 3 2 1

Published simultaneously in Canada by Little, Brown & Company (Canada) Limited

ISBN 0-316-71967-6
Library of Congress Catalog Card Number 90-050348

1

"Hum it in there!" Breezy Hawk shouted from the dugout. "Come on, Joey! One more out!" she screamed at the pitcher, her dark eyes flashing. "These guys are nothing!"

On the mound, Joey Carpenter pulled his cap down over his close-cropped brown hair and shook his head at the catcher.

"What's he doing?" Kim Yardley asked, following her best friend Breezy's gaze.

"He's shaking off the catcher's signal," Breezy answered, pulling on the brim of her baseball hat in disgust. She looked over at Rob Simpson who was crouched behind the batter. "Rob's calling a great game. What in the world does Joey think he's doing?"

"He's too much," Kim snorted, pushing her red bangs out of her eyes. "Just because he's the coach's son, he thinks he can get away with anything! Does Joey think his fastball is *that* good?"

"Well, it usually is," Breezy admitted. "But Peter

Tolhurst is the best slugger in the league." She tightened her already too-tight, long, dark blonde ponytail. "He eats fastballs for breakfast. We're tied with Mel's Auto Body, the team that only happened to have won the division championship last year, and Joey's shaking off the signals. . . ."

She let her voice trail off as she watched Joey go into his windup. He threw one right down the center of the plate. Peter's bat was a blur as he connected with the pitch. The ball took off like a shot out to centerfield. Butch Jacobs, the centerfielder, took two steps back to the wall and then stopped. He watched as the ball kept rising and cleared the fence. It didn't look as if it was ever going to come down.

Breezy threw her glove to the ground in disgust. "I don't believe it! What was Joey doing? He's better than that!" She kicked the dirt with her cleats. She couldn't imagine why Joey would have thrown a hitter like Peter Tolhurst a fastball right down the center of the plate—not even aiming for an outside corner!

Kim whistled in admiration. "That was some blast!" she said. "Anything hit that high should have a flight attendant on it!"

Peter rounded the bases at a slow trot. As he jogged down the third base line, he looked in the girls' direction as they stood watching, and he grinned right at Breezy.

"You know, I think he likes you," Kim said.

"What?!" Breezy yelped.

"I think he likes you," Kim repeated. "You like him, don't you? He is really cute."

"I do not!" Breezy said sharply. That was the most ridiculous thing she had ever heard. "I just think he's a good baseball player."

Kim smiled at her. "Right," she said. Breezy could tell Kim didn't believe her. But, Peter liking her—it was off the wall. No way!

As soon as Peter crossed home plate, he was totally surrounded by his teammates. Breezy looked up at the scoreboard and watched as the score changed: Mel's Auto Body-1, Mitchell Lumber-0.

Great, she thought. Now they were losing. She was going to have to really concentrate to get them back into the game next inning. That was, of course, *if* Coach Carpenter let her pitch. In the first game of the pre-season last week, the coach had put Brian Jones in to pitch the second half. Breezy thought Brian was an O.K. guy, but he couldn't pitch his way out of a paper bag. But *she* was a good pitcher. In fact, she was a great pitcher—at least 10 times better than Brian, and probably just as good as, if not better, than Joey. But Breezy spent all her time on the bench. Ever since she had joined the Eastern Maryland Baseball League (known as Emblem) last year when she was 11, she had been left on the bench. Kim had been, too, even though she was so good at shortstop that she could almost cover second base herself after she fielded the ball near third. It was totally unfair.

"Come on, Joey!" a high-pitched voice screamed from the stands.

Kim and Breezy looked at each other. "Lindsay," Breezy said in disgust. Lindsay Cunningham was in seventh grade with them at Eleanor Roosevelt Junior High. There was not a lot of love lost between the two girls. In fact, Breezy couldn't stand Lindsay, who walked around Roosevelt as if she were a princess or something. And the fact that she was Joey Carpenter's girlfriend did nothing to make her more acceptable to Breezy.

"There she is," Kim stated, pointing to the end of the bleachers beyond the dugout. "She makes me sick."

Breezy followed Kim's stare. Lindsay was surrounded by her clique. These were all girls who wanted to be popular like Lindsay, so they followed her everywhere. Breezy could not understand the attraction. She had no clue why anyone would want to fall all over themselves trying to impress Lindsay. Breezy looked at her. Lindsay's long, white-blonde hair was in a high ponytail and she was wearing a pink mini-skirt and a matching pink tank top. She almost always wore pink. Breezy hated pink.

"Isn't that Jazz with Lindsay?" Kim asked. She squinted her brown eyes as she tried to get a better look.

Breezy turned her attention back to the game. She couldn't care less what her cousin Jasmine Jaffe, known as Jazz, was doing with Lindsay Cunningham. Breezy and Jazz had absolutely nothing in common, even if they

4

were related. Talking to Jazz was a total waste of time as far as Breezy was concerned. Jazz wasn't interested in sports at all! Unbelieveable. All she wanted to talk about was boys—how cute so-and-so was, and what a hunk such-and-such was. It was all really stupid in Breezy's eyes.

"Aarrgh!" Breezy screamed as Joey threw a pitch to the next hitter, Jim Robbins. "That ball bounced before it reached the plate!" Breezy said to Kim, who nodded in agreement. "This is totally ridiculous!"

Joey's next three pitches were strikes. He finally seemed to find his groove.

"Now why couldn't he do that before?" Kim asked Breezy as the Mitchell Lumber team headed into the dugout.

"Beats me," Breezy replied.

"Do you think we'll get to bat now?" Kim asked.

"We'd better," Breezy said firmly, as she pulled her batting glove out of the back pocket of her pants and jammed it on her left hand.

It was the top of the fourth inning. Emblem games were six innings long, and since pitchers couldn't pitch more than six innings in a week, Coach Carpenter almost always rotated players at the fourth inning.

Breezy stood up and went to look for her favorite bat. It was one of the few wooden ones left. Breezy hated the new aluminum ones. They didn't make the same satisfying sound when she hit the ball.

Coach Carpenter was the last one into the dugout by the time he waddled over from where he had been standing next to first base. Breezy couldn't understand why he didn't stay in the dugout like most coaches did when their team was on the field. He probably just wanted to make sure his players saw him glare at them anytime one of them made an error.

"Here's the lineup, boys," Coach Carpenter wheezed at the team. The coach was a huge man. His belly hung way out over his pants. His uniform was too small for him, so his stomach always showed at the bottom of his jersey. And he was constantly chomping on a cigar. Breezy felt sick just looking at him. She had absolutely no patience with people who didn't take care of their bodies. She knew Coach Carpenter was a prime candidate for an early heart attack if he didn't do something soon. Before her grandfather died of a heart attack last year, his stomach had looked a lot like her coach's.

"Boys?" Kim questioned under her breath to Breezy. They looked at each other. Breezy and Kim both hated it when the coach called everyone boys. The two of them were as good as any of the boys out there, and better than most, so they didn't like it when the coach made them feel invisible.

The coach ran down the lineup. Surprise, surprise, Breezy thought. Brian Jones was pitching and Kevin Jordan was still at shortstop.

"Kevin's got lead feet," Kim muttered.

"What was that?" Coach Carpenter asked, turning to the end of the bench where Breezy and Kim were sitting.

"Nothing," Kim said, at the same time as Joey said, "Something about Kevin's feet."

Joey turned and sneered at Breezy. Breezy could feel herself getting really angry. Her brothers joked that when she got angry they could see the smoke coming out of her ears. It was bad enough that she and Kim were still on the bench, but now Joey was causing trouble.

"What about my feet?" Kevin asked Kim. He pushed his blond bangs out of his eyes. Breezy had no idea how Kevin could play with all that hair in his eyes all the time

"Well?" Joey prodded. Breezy almost hoped that Joey would pick a fight. A fight was just what she needed. But everyone on the team liked Kim—except Joey and his father. Breezy knew that Kevin wouldn't yell at Kim no matter what Kim said.

Kim laughed. "I just said you've got big feet, Kevin," she said, punching him on the arm.

Kevin smiled and looked down at his size-10 cleats. His "boats" were the joke of the league. Kevin smiled. "Only you can get away with it, Yardley," he said, tugging on one of her red braids. Kim giggled.

Joey turned toward Kevin. "That's not what I heard," he said.

"Don't worry about it," Kevin replied, bending down to find his batting helmet.

"Joey!!" Coach Carpenter yelled. "What's going on

with those girls down there?"

"Kim was making cracks," Joey answered, getting up and walking over to his father.

"Keep your mind on the game, Yardley," the coach screamed at Kim. "Isn't that just like a girl!" He turned back to his clipboard.

"He makes me so mad!" Breezy said through gritted teeth.

"Breeze, come on," Kim said. "Calm down. The smoke's coming out of your ears."

Breezy was so angry by then that she barely heard what Kim was saying. Breezy couldn't remember the last time she had been this mad about anything. Sure, she had gotten kind of mad at that swimming meet two weeks ago when the officials claimed that she had false-started, but it wasn't even close to this.

"I'm sick and tired of this whole thing!" Breezy said. "I'm going to forget how to pitch if I don't get in a game soon!"

"Please, Breezy," Kim said and laughed. "You play baseball in your sleep. There's no way you'll ever forget how to hum a fastball in there."

"He shouldn't lean back so much," Breezy suddenly said, changing the subject. Her attention had returned to the field. She was talking about Kevin, who was up first. He stood at the plate completely flat-footed. The pitch came whizzing past him, and Kevin swung after the ball had already hit the catcher's mitt.

"That wasn't even that fast," Kim said, squinting toward home plate.

"No," Breezy agreed. "But Kevin's always behind because he doesn't know how to shift his weight forward. He just keeps himself over that back foot. There's no way he'll ever be able to get around in time." Breezy practically lived and breathed baseball during the season. There was little she didn't know about playing the game.

Breezy's prediction came true, as Kevin swung too late on the next two pitches and was out one-two-three.

Kim moaned and buried her face in her hand. "We'll never get that run back at this rate. Who's up next?"

"Butch," Breezy answered. "Maybe he'll get something going." Butch swung his bat from side to side as he stepped up to the batter's box. He pulled the brim of his helmet down and glared at the pitcher.

"I think he's really mad about that run," Kim said, observing him. "He looks ready to belt it out of here."

The first pitch came over way inside. Butch took it for ball one.

"Good eye!" Breezy yelled.

"Come on, Butch!" Kim screamed. "You can do it!"

Butch stepped out of the batter's box and tapped his cleats with the end of the bat. He took off his helmet, straightened his cap, put his helmet back on and stepped up to the plate again. The pitch came in fast and on the outside corner. Butch caught a piece of it, but popped it

9

up right to the third baseman, who caught it easily. Two outs.

Kim groaned again. She buried her face in her hands. "Tell me when it's over," she said to Breezy. "Who's up now?"

"Brian Jones," Breezy said. Brian was even worse at hitting than he was at pitching. Breezy didn't get it. Why didn't the coach put her in? She wasn't a slugger or anything, but she usually got on base at least.

The infield started chattering, "Easy out, easy out."

Brian looked nervous as he stepped up to the plate. He went into his crouch hesitantly and looked at the pitcher.

"It looks like we're not going to get a thing going this inning," Breezy stated in disgust. "Why does he have to look like he's giving up before the pitcher even throws the ball? Why does Brian even bother?"

"Leave him alone, Breezy," Kim said. "Everybody knows he doesn't even want to play baseball. He'd rather be inside playing chess or something. His father makes him play."

"Well why does he have to pitch? Why can't he play rightfield?" Breezy asked, turning toward Kim.

Breezy and Kim watched as the first pitch whizzed in for a strike right up the middle. Brian hadn't even moved his bat.

"Coach Carpenter wouldn't put us in even if he had only eight players," Kim said, shaking her head. "I don't have anything against Brian. I mean, I like Brian. But I don't know what the coach has against us."

"We're girls!" Breezy exclaimed. "A fate worse than death. Is he afraid I'll out-pitch his precious Joey or what?"

"Maybe," Kim agreed, and then groaned. Brian didn't move for the next two pitches. Another out. The side was retired and the boys all scrambled for their gloves and rushed out to the field. Only Breezy, Kim, Rob and John Richie were left in the dugout. As soon as Rob finished buckling his shin and chest pads, he was back behind the plate. John was the backup centerfielder, but he didn't get to play that often. Butch was really good.

"I can't take this anymore!" Breezy suddenly shouted. "I've had it!" She stood up and started pacing back and forth in front of the bench.

"Why don't you just sit down and shut up, Hawk," John practically ordered. "You're really starting to bother me."

Breezy kicked a few of the bats lying on the ground and whirled around to face John. Kim jumped up and grabbed Breezy's arm. "Calm down, Breeze," Kim said, pulling her over to the bench. Breezy didn't feel as if she would ever calm down, though. She was totally sick of the guys on the team ordering her around. Brian walked the first two Mel's Auto Body batters in just eight pitches. The smoke was definitely coming out of Breezy's ears now. "I can't watch anymore," she mumbled, rubbing her eyes. The thump of a ball caught Breezy's attention. She glanced over at John, who was throwing a ball up and catching it in his glove. He saw her looking at him and sneered back as he threw his ball at the chain link fence in front of the dugout. Breezy turned her attention back to the game.

Suddenly, the batter swung and hit the ball straight at the shortstop. At the same time, John again threw his ball at the chain link fence—but he threw too high and the ball sailed over the fence and onto the field. The third baseman went for John's ball, and the shortstop covered the ball just hit by the batter. Both players threw their balls at the first baseman at the same time. The first baseman didn't know what to do, and let both balls go by.

"Safe!" the ump shouted, crossing his arms back and forth in front of his body as the batter crossed first base.

"What?" Coach Carpenter screamed, running up to the ump. "There were too many balls on the field! That can't be legal!"

"He's still safe," the ump insisted. "Besides, that ball came from your dugout."

"*WHAT?!*" the coach yelled again, even louder. "Those darn girls!"

"Uh, oh," Kim said under her breath as she looked at Breezy. Breezy's jaw was jutting forward, and her eyes were dark with anger. She was not going to take anything from the coach.

"Who threw that ball?" the coach asked, moving in front of the dugout. John didn't say a thing. In fact, he didn't move. "I said, *who threw that ball?*"

John was as still as a statue. Coach Carpenter stalked over and stood right in front of the dugout. He pointed at Kim and Breezy. "Get over here!" he yelled, his beefy face bright red.

Kim stood up automatically. Breezy got to her feet slowly. The coach had a lot of nerve blaming them for something John had done.

"NOW!" Coach Carpenter screamed. The veins on his forehead were standing out so much they looked as if they were going to burst any second.

Kim scrambled up the steps and out on the field. Breezy didn't want her friend to face the angry coach alone, so she followed her. "You better tell him you did it," she said under her breath to John as she passed by. John just stared at his glove as if he had never seen anything like it before. Breezy walked out onto the field and right up to the coach.

"You girls are always causing trouble . . ." Coach Carpenter began.

"We didn't do it!" Breezy cut him off, not even noticing that the game had not resumed and that both teams, in fact everyone in the area, was watching their confrontation. The only thing Breezy saw out of the corner of her eye was Joey grinning as he walked in from leftfield. That made her even madder.

Coach Carpenter sputtered and opened his mouth.

"John did it!" Kim added, stepping out from behind Breezy.

"I can't believe you're trying to blame John," Joey called out as he walked up behind his father. "I saw you girls throw the ball. I can't believe you'd lie to save yourselves."

Shocked into silence momentarily, Breezy couldn't believe that Joey was lying. She glared at him. He sneered back.

"You two have disrupted my team for the last time!" the coach yelled. "You've been nothing but trouble since the season started. You're both benched!"

Breezy couldn't help herself—she started laughing. The whole thing was so ridiculous. They were being benched for something they hadn't done. And meanwhile, they had both been on the bench for over a year now. Coach Carpenter was very angry. He was chomping on his cigar so furiously that little bits were flying all over the place.

"Did you hear me?" he screamed, putting his face right up to Breezy's.

Breezy didn't even flinch. "We've been benched since we joined this stupid league!" she yelled back. "Besides, we didn't throw the ball in the first place! You can't bench me anymore—I quit!"

"Me, too!" Kim echoed.

The coach's mouth dropped open and his cigar fell to

the ground. Breezy turned on her heel and stomped back to the dugout to get her bat. Kim followed.

"You really are a jerk!" Breezy yelled at John, grabbing her glove.

"Well, at least I won't have to see *you* anymore!" he retorted. "You're out of here!"

Breezy stormed back toward the field. Joey was still standing behind his father, laughing. "Go back to your Barbie dolls!" he said.

Dragging Kim out of the ballpark, Breezy spun around and yelled at Joey, "You're just scared of my fastball, Joey Carpenter! You'll be sorry when it comes whizzing by you!"

2

"Morning," Breezy mumbled on Monday morning as she rushed into the kitchen. She walked over to the refrigerator and opened the door.

"Good morning, Amy," Mrs. Hawk greeted her from over by the stove. "What do you want for breakfast?"

Breezy looked around the door at her mother. Mrs. Hawk definitely didn't look as if she had four kids. In fact, a lot of people thought she was Breezy's older sister. Her hair was the same dark blonde as Breezy's and she always wore it in a ponytail. And Mrs. Hawk was always running in road races, so she was in great shape.

Wrinkling her nose at the thought of a big breakfast, Breezy reached into the refrigerator for a carton of milk. "I'm really in kind of a rush, Mom," Breezy answered, opening the carton and taking a swig of milk.

"Amy, how many times do I have to tell you to use a glass?" her mother scolded, waving a spatula. "You're as bad as your brothers."

Breezy shrugged and put the milk back in the

refrigerator. This was definitely nothing new.

Danny, Breezy's nine-year-old brother, suddenly came running into the kitchen and threw himself on the bench of the trestle table. "I want pancakes," he announced to his mother.

"Good morning, Danny," Mrs. Hawk said, pouring batter into a skillet. She put a plate and a glass of orange juice in front of Danny and turned toward Breezy. "Amy, how many do you want?"

"I've got to run, Mom," Breezy replied, grabbing an apple. She walked behind Danny and picked up his glass of juice. Taking a slug of it, she patted Danny's dark blond crew cut. "Have a good day, kiddo," she whispered, and then walked out the door.

"Amy!" her mother called after her. "Breakfast is the most important meal of the day!"

Biting into the apple, Breezy picked up her knapsack and opened the front door. "See you later, Mom!" she called out and shut the door behind her. She grabbed her bike from the garage and started pedaling toward school.

Kim was waiting for her by the front doors when Breezy got there. They walked inside and stopped by the bulletin board across from the office. The hallways were pretty empty because there were still 15 minutes before the first bell rang for homeroom. Breezy wanted to get the announcement about her new baseball team up on the bulletin board before anyone else got to school.

Breezy grabbed a chair from a nearby classroom and

pulled it over in front of the bulletin board. She pulled a sign out of her knapsack and Kim handed her a few thumbtacks.

"That's crooked, Breezy," Kim said from behind her friend. "Lift the left side a little bit more."

"Like this?" Breezy asked.

"Still crooked," Kim stated, a little impatiently.

"What are you talking about?" Breezy asked. "Give me a break! It's fine the way it is. Besides, my arms are killing me from holding it up." She put the final tacks in and jumped off the chair, landing next to Kim. Breezy groaned. Kim was right. The sign was still crooked.

"At least everyone will see the sign here," Breezy said. "I bet a lot of people will show up this afternoon to join our team."

"I hope we get at least nine girls," Kim answered, looking up at the sign about the baseball meeting.

"Come on, Kim," Breezy said confidently. "Of course we will. Don't even worry about it."

Suddenly, from behind them, Breezy and Kim heard Lindsay Cunningham reading their sign in her annoying voice: "TIRED OF SITTING ON THE BENCH? GIRLS-ONLY BASEBALL TEAM MEETING AT THE FIREMAN'S FIELD AT 3 O'CLOCK." They turned around and saw Lindsay standing right behind them, with Joey. Her white-blonde hair was in a French braid, and she was wearing pale pink leggings, pink Keds and a pink and mint green striped sweater. Breezy couldn't remember ever seeing Lindsay in any other color but pink. Lindsay's crowd was there too, of course.

"All-girls team?" Joey added snidely. He was wearing what he always wore—jeans, untied high-top sneakers and a black-and-red rugby shirt. His brown hair was slicked back with gel. First of all, Breezy couldn't understand why people wore sneakers untied. Wouldn't the shoes fall off or the laces get tangled all the time? Second, she had no idea why a guy would put gel in his hair. "I hope you're not planning on playing against the boys," Joey continued. "An all-girls team wouldn't have a prayer—especially with you pitching."

Joey and Lindsay cracked up. Lindsay's friends giggled, too. Breezy noticed that her boy-crazy cousin Jazz wasn't with them.

"I wouldn't talk, Joey," Breezy said, taking a step toward him. "*You're* the one who lost the game for us yesterday," she added, shaking her finger in his face.

"*Us*?" Joey asked, waving her off. "What do you mean *us*? You're not on the team. You don't have a team anymore."

"We're starting our own team," Kim cut in. "And you can't stop us. Mr. Egan said that we have until Friday to get a team and a sponsor. The season doesn't really start until Saturday."

"You're not even going to get nine players together by Friday," Lindsay said snidely. "Girls who want to play baseball just want to be boys." She looked Breezy and Kim up and down, curling her lip.

"Really," Beth Douglas agreed with Lindsay. Beth always agreed with Lindsay. That's probably why they have been best friends for so long, Breezy figured. She didn't think Beth had ever had an original thought in her life. Beth always said, "Lindsay says."

"They even dress like boys," Lindsay said. The other girls nodded in agreement.

Breezy looked down at the Washington Redskins jersey that was hanging almost to her knees. She was proud of that jersey. Former quarterback Joe Theisman had given it to her father, who was a police detective, at some policemen's benefit dinner. She was wearing her favorite red-and-white Nike high tops. Looking over her shoulder at Kim, Breezy saw her best friend hastily tucking her T-shirt into her jeans. What did Lindsay mean, they dressed like boys? Just because they didn't wear pink?

"We do not," Kim protested, putting her hands on her hips.

"No matter what you look like," Joey said, leaning toward Breezy so that he was practically breathing in her face, "it's not going to help you play baseball."

"We'll just have to wait and see, Carpenter," Breezy snapped, her eyes never leaving Joey's face. Breezy felt as if the two of them were in a staring contest like the ones she used to have with her brothers when she was little. There was no way she was going to look away first.

The halls were starting to fill with kids rushing to their lockers, but Breezy didn't even notice. The warning bell rang, and she didn't budge. "Breezy, Breezy," Kim said, tugging on her friend's sleeve. "We've got to get moving. We're going to be late for homeroom." Breezy still didn't look away from Joey.

"Joey," Lindsay whined. "Come on, I don't want to get in trouble." She pulled Joey's arm, and he looked away from Breezy. Breezy smiled tightly. She had won. Joey really was a wuss. Breezy then allowed Kim to drag her down the hall toward their lockers.

"He makes me so mad!" Kim said once they got to Breezy's locker. "He thinks he's so great."

"I can't wait to see his face when I strike him out," Breezy answered, pulling her locker open. "He's such a jerk. Girls can do anything boys can. Where's my English book?" she asked as she started digging around in her locker, which was a total mess. Books and papers were jumbled up every which way. Pulling everything out and onto the floor, Breezy looked up at Kim. "You better get going. I may be here awhile," she said with a groan.

Kim nodded and headed down the hall. "I'll see you at lunch, O.K.?" Kim called over her shoulder.

Breezy bent down to go through the bottom of her locker. Where in the world was that book? She knew she hadn't left it at home. Feeling a tap on her shoulder, Breezy looked up, startled.

"Hey," Peter Tolhurst greeted her.

Looking up at Peter, all she could think about was what Kim had said at the game about him liking her. Breezy just nodded. Somehow she couldn't seem to say anything. She guessed he was cute and all. Peter had dark brown hair that was longer in the back and curled up over the collar of his emerald green T-shirt, which Breezy suddenly noticed matched his green eyes perfectly. His T-shirt was tucked into a pair of ratty old Levi's and he was wearing a pair of black basketball sneakers. Peter was even better at basketball than baseball. And Breezy thought he was the best slugger in Emblem.

"How's it going?" Peter continued. "What are you looking for?"

Breezy looked down at the floor. Practically her entire locker was spread out in the hallway in front of her. "My English book," she mumbled.

Peter reached over her and pulled a book off the top shelf of her locker. "This it?" he asked, grinning.

Breezy stood up, but Peter didn't step back. His face was only a few inches in front of hers. She felt her cheeks get warm and she realized she was blushing. What was the matter with her? Nothing made her blush—especially not a boy. Anyway, she had known Peter practically forever.

Then Peter handed her the book, bent down and started shoveling all the papers and books on the floor back into her locker. Breezy finally got moving and helped Peter shove the last of her junk back into her locker. She stood up and slammed the locker shut. "Thanks," Breezy muttered. She was going to kill Kim. If Kim hadn't mentioned anything about Peter liking her, she never would have been this nervous now.

"No prob," he replied. "Hey, I'm sorry about what happened at the game yesterday."

"That's O.K.," Breezy said in a soft voice. "Coach Carpenter made me so mad . . . ."

"Me, too," Peter agreed, cutting her off. "Can I walk with you to homeroom?"

Now Breezy was really confused. Why was he asking her that? They were both in the same homeroom. What was she going to say—no, walk by yourself? Feeling more and more uncomfortable, Breezy just nodded and she and Peter started off toward their classroom.

"So what's this I hear about a new team?" Peter asked, keeping in step with her. "Are you really starting your own?"

"Yeah," Breezy answered, turning up the stairs. "It's only for girls."

"That's sexist," Peter replied. Breezy felt her spine stiffen. She turned toward him ready to tell him off, but saw that he was grinning. "Gotcha! I'm just kidding. I think that's great. It made me mad last year when our coach never played any of the girls on our team."

"Well, now we'll all be playing—" Breezy began heatedly.

"I know, I know," Peter cut her off, laughing. "And I

23

can't wait to hit against you. I hear you're a good pitcher."

"I am," Breezy agreed, just as the final bell rang. Luckily, they were right outside the door to their classroom. No one was seated yet and everyone was still talking. The two of them were able to slip right in without even being noticed. Breezy sighed with relief as she slipped into her seat. Detention would have been all she needed.

The morning flew by for Breezy. Everyone had something to say about her team, though. And a lot of the responses were definitely not good. But at least it took her mind off the Peter situation. He had asked to walk her to her first class, and he had even told Joey to shut up when he made a crack about Breezy in the hallway. Breezy hadn't heard what Joey said, but Peter was all over him before he had even finished talking. It was really weird.

Breezy was late for math class after lunch. She had turned her locker upside down and still couldn't find last night's homework. It must have gotten lost when she was looking for her English book that morning. After she finally unburied it, she ran down the hall at full speed, but didn't make it. The bell rang just as she crashed into the silent classroom.

"I'm glad you could honor us with your presence, Miss Hawk," Mr. Browne, the math teacher, greeted her, tapping his desk with a piece of chalk.

"She was probably out recruiting some dorks for her team," Sean Dunphy called out from the second row.

The class giggled. Breezy's face flamed, as she stalked to her desk in the back of the room. She threw herself in her seat and glared at Mr. Browne. Mr. Browne loved to nail her when she was a few seconds late. He hardly ever yelled at the boys, though. Once she had answered a question without raising her hand first, and Mr. Browne had given her a 10-minute lecture about proper classroom manners.

"Amy, you're starting a baseball team?" the teacher asked. That was another thing about Mr. Browne. He always called her Amy. She hated being called Amy, even though it was her real name.

"It's only for girls," Sean called out again, as if that fact was the funniest thing in the world.

Mr. Browne laughed as he walked up and down the aisles. Breezy clenched her fists. Of course, Mr. Browne wasn't telling the *boys* about classroom manners.

"There aren't even nine girls in this whole school who know how to play baseball," called out Chuck Singer, one of Joey's friends, from the other side of the room.

Breezy's eyes turned dark. She was sick and tired of these stupid cracks. She'd prove them all wrong soon enough. But before Breezy could say a word, Mr. Browne said, "Now that's an interesting math question, Mr. Singer."

He walked over to Breezy's desk. Mr. Browne tapped

his chalk on her desk. "Tell me, Miss Hawk," he said, smiling down at her. "Let's see how well you learned your percentages this weekend. Let's say there are only eight girls in the whole seventh grade who can play baseball . . . ."

"Too many! Too many!" a few boys called out.

"O.K., seven girls . . . "

Breezy was getting really mad now. Mr. Browne was as bad as her coach was—her ex-coach, that is.

"Well, let's make it six," Mr. Browne continued. "And there are 120 girls in the class. What percentage of girls in the seventh grade can play baseball?"

Breezy was so mad she couldn't even think. "I'm waiting, Miss Hawk," Mr. Browne said, still tapping his chalk on her desk. "What's your first step?"

"It's five percent," Crystal Joseph called out from the front row, rescuing Breezy. The black girl had just moved to Hampstead, Maryland, from Cleveland a month before. She was in Breezy's science, English and social studies classes, too. The only time she'd ever heard Crystal say anything was when someone specifically asked her a question. All Breezy really knew about her was that she was a dancer and walked with her feet pointed out and took ballet classes all the time.

Mr. Browne whirled around. "So, only *five percent* of the girls in the seventh grade can play baseball, Miss Joseph?" the teacher asked. "How did you come to that conclusion?"

Crystal looked down at her notebook. "Six divided by 120 times . . ." her voice trailed off. Her curly black hair was pulled back into a neat, tight braid.

"What?" he asked. "Speak louder so the entire class can hear."

"Times 100," Crystal stammered, finally looking up from her notebook.

"Very good, Miss Joseph," Mr. Browne commented. He turned back to the board.

Breezy looked at Crystal, who swiveled in her chair. A shy smile crept across her face. Breezy grinned back. Math was definitely not Breezy's best subject. She had had no clue as to how to solve the problem, and she was more than glad that Crystal had answered the question for her. It was strange, though, that Mr. Browne hadn't yelled at Crystal for calling out the answer.

After class, Breezy had to go back to her locker before science to pick up her lab book. "Hi," Crystal said softly, catching up with Breezy.

"Hey, Crystal," Breezy replied, looking up at her. She had never stood next to Crystal before, so she hadn't realized just how tall she was. Breezy only came up to Crystal's nose. Breezy stopped in front of her locker and twirled the combination lock. "Thanks for answering that stupid problem."

Crystal just nodded. Breezy thought she looked as if she wanted to say something else, but couldn't seem to get the words out.

When Breezy opened her locker, she breathed a sigh of relief. She could see her science book on the bottom. Now she wouldn't have to drag everything out on the floor again. She really had to clean out her locker sometime. She grabbed the notebook and shut the locker, and then turned and started walking toward science class.

"I couldn't believe what he was saying about your baseball team, Breezy," Crystal said suddenly, coming up beside Breezy.

"He is such a jerk!" Breezy exclaimed. "I can't stand how he treats the girls in that class!"

"I know," Crystal agreed. They headed down the stairs together. "Listen . . ." she began.

"Yeah?" Breezy prompted. She turned down the hall, and paused in front of their classroom. This girl Crystal really had a hard time talking or something. Kim was always yelling at Breezy for interrupting, so Breezy bit her tongue, waiting for Crystal to continue.

"I was wondering if . . ." Crystal went on.

"What?" Breezy prodded.

"If I could maybe join your team even if I've never played baseball but I'm a fast learner and I'm sure I'd pick it up quickly," Crystal blurted out in a rush, the words practically running together.

"I guess so," Breezy responded, trying to sound enthusiastic. Breezy really wanted to have a *good* team, and she couldn't if the players didn't know how to play. Then again, the reason she wanted to start her own team was so all of the girls who couldn't play in Emblem would be able to play. "Yeah, sure," she added with a smile.

"I think it's great that you're starting this team, Breezy," Crystal added.

Breezy pushed open the door to the science lab and walked inside. Crystal followed. As Crystal made her way to the far side of the room, Breezy called out to her, "We're meeting at 3 o'clock at the Fireman's Field, O.K.?"

Crystal nodded as she sat down. Breezy noticed that she was smiling—a really big smile. Breezy didn't think she had ever seen Crystal smile like that before.

Mrs. Rosen walked into the classroom just then carrying a jar of dead frogs. At least science class would be interesting, Breezy thought. She could definitely get into something like dissecting frogs. It would keep her mind off her first team meeting, which was only an hour away. Breezy had no idea who would actually show up. Everybody had been talking about it, but Crystal was the only one who had promised to actually be there. She hoped that some girls would show up who knew how to play. Otherwise, it would be a really long season.

3

"I can't believe no one else showed up!" Breezy ex-claimed angrily two hours later at the Neptune Diner. Her aunt and uncle owned the diner and Breezy and Kim spent a lot of time there, even if it meant seeing Breezy's cousin, Jazz, who was usually hanging around the place. Breezy slurped up the last of her chocolate shake. She had a real weakness for chocolate.

"Well," Kim said. "We really didn't give anyone much notice. You can't expect everyone to be able to come on the exact same day you announce it, can you?" She swirled the ice cubes in her soda.

"I'm sure more people will come to the next practice," Crystal added, spearing a piece of lettuce with her fork.

"That's all you're eating?" Breezy asked, pointing to the small tossed salad in front of Crystal.

"Well, I have to watch what I eat," Crystal explained. "Ballet dancers are really thin."

"What are you talking about?" Kim asked. She threw one of her red braids over her shoulder so it wouldn't fall into the sandwich in front of her. "You're such a twig, Crystal!" Kim shook her head in disbelief. Breezy grabbed some of Kim's French fries and jammed them in her mouth.

"Hey!" Kim exclaimed, slapping Breezy's hand. "Get your own. Anyway, Crystal, it's not like you've got to watch your weight for baseball. It doesn't matter what you look like—it's all in the swing." She giggled, and moved her fries in front of her.

"I still can't believe no one showed up," Breezy repeated, groaning. "I think I need another milkshake."

"We've got until Friday," Kim said, consoling her friend.

"I know. I'm sure we'll have no problem, but . . ." Breezy's voice trailed off after she noticed someone standing over them.

"This booth looks like depression city," said Eddie Andrews. Eddie worked in the diner every afternoon. He was studying law enforcement and he planned to go to the state trooper academy. Breezy's father was helping him out. Practically every girl in town was in love with Eddie. He was 27, had short black curly hair and hazel eyes. He lifted weights in his spare time, so he was in good shape, too. Breezy didn't remember him ever having a steady girlfriend, though. Mrs. Hawk said he was a "confirmed bachelor," whatever that was. "Can I get you all anything?" Eddie continued, flashing the girls one of his most dazzling smiles. Kim giggled.

"I'll have another chocolate," Breezy said, handing Eddie her empty glass. Her mother would probably kill her, but she really felt that she *had* to have another shake.

"Two in one day?" he asked. "It must have been pretty bad."

"Yeah, well, it'll get better," Breezy answered confidently. She was certainly not going to let one setback make her give up.

"Hey, who's this?" Eddie asked, looking at Crystal with interest. "I know I've never met you before because I definitely would have remembered."

Crystal blushed and looked down at her salad. "This is Crystal Joseph," Kim said. "She's new."

"Where are you from?" Eddie asked, sitting down in the booth next to Breezy. Breezy glared at him. She wanted her milkshake. "Cleveland," Crystal answered. "We moved here a month ago."

"Hey!" Eddie exclaimed. "Do you have a brother named Arnie?"

"Yes," Crystal replied, taking a sip of water. "And one named Kyle."

"Right, I know them," Eddie said. "Your father is going to be the football coach at the high school. I'm going to help out with games on the weekends." He stood up and grinned at Breezy. "I know, I know. You want your shake. Don't worry, it's on its way." He turned toward Kim. "You don't want anything, do you, Shorty?" he asked, tweaking on one of her braids. She giggled and shook her head. He laughed one more time, and headed back to the kitchen.

"He's *sooo* cute," Kim said, sighing as she watched him go.

"He's too old for you," Breezy said quickly. Kim frowned at her friend and slurped her soda. "Oh, great!" Breezy exclaimed, looking at the door.

Kim and Crystal followed her stare. There was Lindsay Cunningham with her usual crowd. "Oh, look who's here!" Lindsay said sarcastically. "It's the famous all-girls team that's going to show the boys how to play baseball."

Breezy clenched her fists. Lindsay always knew exactly how to get her mad. But Breezy was determined to ignore her.

"And how was practice today?" Lindsay went on, walking by Breezy's booth. "I bet you got a *big* turnout."

Breezy wondered if they already knew that no one had shown up. But that was so typical of Lindsay. She usually knew things practically before they happened. It was one of her most annoying traits.

"Oh, I see you're hanging out with the 'duck,' now," Lindsay said, continuing her attack on the girls, this time focusing on Crystal. Lindsay and her friends started walking toward a booth in the back with their toes pointed out, imitating Crystal's walk. Like many dancers, Crystal walked with her toes and knees pointed out.

Breezy stood up, but Kim grabbed her arm and pulled

her down. Breezy looked at Crystal, who was staring straight down at her salad. She shook Kim off and stood up again. "She's not worth it, Breezy," Crystal said quietly. "If you fight with her, she'll just be getting the attention she wants. That's probably why she bugs you all the time—she knows you'll react. And she's obviously threatened by you because you're so strong."

Breezy's mouth dropped open. "You sound like a psychiatrist, Crystal," Breezy said. "Anyway, the point is that I hate her as much as she hates me. It's been like that since first grade."

But Breezy knew Crystal was right, so she just gritted her teeth and stayed right where she was. When Eddie brought her shake over, she toyed with the idea of marching over to Lindsay's table and dumping it over her head. No matter what, Breezy decided she was going to show Lindsay and her crowd. Her team was going to be the best in Emblem. Breezy Hawk had never been a quitter, and she was not about to start now.

4

"Breezy, wait up!" Kim shouted the next day as she ran to catch up with her friend. The halls were packed with junior-high students on their way to lunch.

"Hurry up! I'm hungry!" Breezy shouted over her shoulder. Kim caught up to her when they got to the end of the lunch line. Luckily, the line was still kind of short. Breezy hated waiting in line for anything—especially lunch.

"I talked to Julie McKay and Andrea Campbell," Breezy announced to Kim as she bent down to tie one of her high-top sneakers. "They're both going to be at the practice tomorrow."

"That's great!" Kim replied enthusiastically. "That makes seven. We're going to have a full team in no time. I told you there would be no problem."

"I told *you*," Breezy contradicted. "I never thought we would have a problem. But seven?" Breezy asked, looking confused. "How do you figure that?"

"Well, you know Sarah Fishman was really into joining this morning . . ." Kim began, picking up a tray.

"She's a pretty good pitcher. She just needs to work on her control," Breezy interrupted. "You forgot your spoon, Kim."

"Thanks," Kim replied, grabbing a spoon. "Now, what was I saying? You're always interrupting me."

"Sor-ry," Breezy teased. "Extra cheese on mine, please," she instructed the cook, pointing at a hamburger. "So?" Breezy turned back toward her friend. "What were you talking about?"

"Sarah talked to Betsy Winston and she wants to join, too . . ." Kim began again.

"Betsy!?" Breezy exclaimed, cutting Kim off once more. "The girl's a total klutz! Can she even throw a ball?"

"You did it again, Breezy!" Kim said loudly, as she grabbed her hamburger off the counter.

"Did what?" Breezy asked. "Are you getting fries? I'll eat the rest of yours if you can't finish them."

"Breezy!" Kim yelled again. "Would you let me get a word out?"

When they got to the end of the line, they grabbed some milk containers, and gave their lunch tickets to the woman at the counter. Then Breezy and Kim scanned the room for an empty table. The cafeteria was already packed with kids.

"There's Crystal. There's some space at her table," Breezy said, pointing to a table in the corner by the window. The two girls walked toward it.

"Hey, shrimp!" Lindsay cried out, as Kim accidentally tripped over one of Lindsay's feet. "Watch it!"

"Well, if you didn't have your big feet sticking way out into the aisle . . ." Kim said as she walked by.

"Hey, C.J.!" Breezy greeted Crystal. Breezy never liked to call anyone by their full names. Almost everyone had a nickname. Crystal was definitely too long a name to be shouting all over the ballfield, so Breezy had decided to call her C.J.

"Hi," Crystal said, as they sat down. They were only two tables away from Lindsay. Lindsay sat at the same table every single day—"her" table.

"I hate eating this close to Lindsay and her crowd," Kim said.

"I know," Breezy agreed. "It gives me indigestion." She glanced over at Lindsay's table. Tons of kids in the seventh grade were always trying to sit at her table. There wasn't even enough room for all of her crowd, much less all of Joey's friends. But Lindsay loved being the center of attention, even if there was no room left to eat.

"How'd we get seven people?" Breezy asked, as she opened her milk carton. "You never finished what you were saying."

"Breezy, you never *let* me finish," Kim complained. "Besides that's seven. You, me, Crystal, Julie, Andrea, Sarah and Betsy."

"Yeah, but Betsy can't play," Breezy persisted, stealing a fry.

"Hey, eat your own!" Kim said, grabbing three of Breezy's.

"I can't play either," Crystal remarked, spooning some of her yogurt into her mouth. "So how come it matters that Betsy can't?"

"Well, I think you're at least athletic," Breezy began. "I mean, you wouldn't trip over your own feet like Betsy does all the time." Breezy stood up and said to Kim, "I don't know how you can eat fries without ketchup. I'll go get some."

"I hate ketchup," Kim shouted to Breezy as her friend walked back to the lunch line.

Five minutes later, Breezy finally made it back into the cafeteria. As she walked back across the room, she suddenly noticed Lindsay and her friends standing in front of Kim and Crystal. Breezy could see that Kim was yelling, but she was too far away to hear what she was saying. Kim's angry face was almost as red as her hair. Even Crystal looked upset. Breezy rushed to get back to the table.

"Isn't it obvious already that no one's going to join your stupid team?" Beth was saying as Breezy got within earshot.

"Really," Lindsay agreed. "I heard your practice was such a big hit, you had to turn people away." She looked at Beth, Gwen and Molly, who always followed Lindsay everywhere. They all giggled on cue.

"Shut up!" Kim shouted back. "We've got all the players we need, Lindsay."

"Right, twerp," Lindsay said. "You expect me to believe that? There aren't enough losers in this school. Just you, the tomboy and this duck." She sneered at Kim and Crystal. Joey and his friends, who had come over to find out what all the commotion was about, started laughing with them.

Kim sputtered, but no words came out of her mouth. Breezy elbowed quickly past Joey as she tried to reach her friends.

Before Breezy could get there, Terry DiSunno stepped in front of Kim and Crystal. "Losers?" Terry asked, her green eyes narrowing as she flung her long, brown hair over her shoulder. She took a menacing step toward Lindsay and glared at her. "Who are you calling a loser? I'm the catcher on this team." Her hands were clenched into fists at her sides.

Breezy finally broke through the crowd. She looked at Kim questioningly. Kim had never said a word to her about Terry DiSunno wanting to be on the team. Terry was one of Emblem's best catchers. She actually got to play sometimes. Even though Breezy was furious with Lindsay, she was excited at the same time. Finally, some-one else who could *really* play!

"*You're* a loser, Lardo," Lindsay retorted. The crowd giggled at the nickname. Terry was big-boned and chunky, and about 10 pounds overweight. She always dressed in really baggy clothes, so she looked even bigger.

Terry took another step toward Lindsay.

"Oh, come on, what are you going to do?" Lindsay asked, backing up a little. "Sit on me?" Everyone cracked up.

"*You're* the loser, Cunningham!" Breezy suddenly shouted, shoving between Terry and Lindsay. "Don't you have anything better to do than rank on our team?"

"Really," Kim agreed, jumping back into the fray. "What's it to you? You're just jealous, aren't you?" she pronounced.

"Make me laugh," Lindsay said with a smug smile on her face, turning to the crowd that had formed around them. Then she flipped her blonde hair over her shoulder and marched out of the cafeteria with her friends following right behind.

Breezy turned to Terry, "I thought you were going to kill her, Terry," she said, laughing.

"Lindsay's really lucky you stepped in," Terry said, her fists still clenched.

"So, you really want to be our catcher?" Kim asked, smiling at the husky girl.

"Well, I guess I don't have a choice," Terry said, grumbling. "I wouldn't give la-de-da Lindsay the satisfaction." With that she turned and walked away.

"Practice is tomorrow after school!" Kim called after

her. "That's great!" she exclaimed to Breezy. "Terry's a great catcher!"

"She can really whack the ball, too," Breezy added. "Now we only need one more player."

5

"You can't all play second base!" Breezy yelled from home plate, looking at the four girls standing near the bag. Crystal, Andrea, Betsy and Julie all wanted to play the same position.

Seven girls had showed up for practice. Sarah was on the pitcher's mound and Kim was at shortstop, but everyone else was on second base. "Three of you are going to have to move!" Breezy continued, walking across the field. No one budged.

"I've played second base in gym," Julie stated loudly, stepping onto the base.

"Well, I want to play it, too," Andrea added, trying to push Julie off the base.

"Me, too," Betsy echoed, trying to fit on the base as well.

"Come on, girls," Kim cut in before Breezy had a chance to say a thing. "Julie's played the base before. Maybe you girls should let her have it." Kim then walked over from her position at shortstop to stand next to

Breezy. They had to get it in hand before it got too ugly.

Breezy shook her head in disgust. This was totally ridiculous, she thought. Betsy didn't even have a glove, and she was fighting to play second base for no reason except that three other people wanted to play it. And why was C.J. so gung-ho on second base? She didn't know the first thing about baseball.

"Isn't the second baseman supposed to play over here?" Crystal asked, moving away from the bag to stand between first and second bases.

"How'd you know that?" Breezy asked in surprise. "I thought you never played before."

"I got a book out of the library last night on how to play," Crystal admitted, tightening the string of her powder blue sweatpants.

"A book?" Breezy asked. She couldn't imagine learning how to do something by reading about it. Breezy looked at the four girls on second base and shook her head again. And where was Terry? She had said she was going to be here. Breezy didn't think she was the kind of person to go back on her word, but . . .

"You know, Crystal," Kim began, pulling her baseball cap down further on her head. "You *really* are tall."

Crystal's head shot up, and she stared at Kim. Her chin jutted forward. "What?" she asked in a hurt voice.

Kim giggled. "I didn't mean that the way it sounded, Crystal," she apologized.

"Well, C.J.," Breezy cut in, knowing exactly what Kim

was getting at, "you really should play *first* base. The tallest person is usually the best for that position. Look at the majors. Just about every first baseman is really tall."

Crystal wrinkled her nose in confusion. "The taller you are, the farther you can stretch to catch the ball," Kim explained.

Crystal was quiet for a moment. Breezy could tell she was thinking about it. "Oh, that makes sense," Crystal finally said, nodding. She smiled at Kim and Breezy and moved over toward first base. "I stand to the left of the base, right?"

"Right," Breezy said. Breezy breathed a sigh of relief. Now they had three positions filled. She still had to figure out what Sarah could do when she wasn't pitching.

"*She's* on this team?" Betsy asked in shock, looking at someone behind Breezy. Breezy whipped around and saw Terry walking toward home plate. Her baseball cap was on backwards and her long brown hair hung down her back. She had on black sweatpants rolled up to her knees, a huge white T-shirt, and black high-top Converse sneakers, unlaced. Terry was carrying a large bag that was so stuffed it couldn't even be zipped. Her cleats dangled from one of the handles.

"I didn't think you were going to show up!" Breezy called across the field.

Terry dropped her bag, and pulled out her catcher's

mask, chest pad and shin guards. She untied her cleats and sat down on home plate to put them on. "I told you I'd be here, I'm here," Terry yelled back. She stood up and started buckling her equipment.

Breezy turned back to the three girls still fighting over the base. "O.K., listen up!" she yelled at them. Terry was obviously ready to practice. Everyone else should be, too. "Julie, you've got second. Betsy, I want you in leftfield. And Andrea, you're on third," she instructed them briskly, tugging on the brim of her baseball cap.

Kim walked back to her position at shortstop, but the other girls didn't move a muscle. "Let's go!" Breezy practically shouted. "We don't have all day!"

Betsy moved first. She started walking slowly out to the field behind Crystal. "Who died and put you in charge?" she called over her shoulder to Breezy.

"I'm the coach!" Breezy yelled at her retreating back. "And Betsy, that's *right*field."

"Oops," Betsy said as she changed directions, grumbling the entire way.

"Third?" Andrea asked Breezy defiantly. "I want to play second."

"Well, Julie's played it before," Breezy said. "Besides, third is just as important, if not more. You have to make sure nothing gets up the line. It's called the 'Hot Corner.'"

"Really?" Andrea asked. Then she started walking past Kim toward her new base.

45

"Finally," Breezy muttered under her breath. They had only wasted a good half-hour fighting. Breezy walked over to the bleachers and picked up a bat and a few balls. She was headed toward home when Betsy called out from leftfield, "I don't have a glove!"

"Well, come get mine!" Breezy shouted. Betsy started walking in toward home. "Geesh!" Breezy exclaimed to herself. Betsy should be jogging in. These girls were going to have to get a little hustle going.

"I'm going to bat these out there!" Breezy called to the team, pointing to the balls at her feet as she stood at home plate. "I want you guys to field them and throw them to first! O.K.? C.J., you throw the balls home after you catch them!"

Breezy tapped the first ball out toward Kim at shortstop. Kim scooped up the grounder neatly and rifled the ball to first base. Crystal was still firmly planted a few feet to the left of the plate, so the ball sailed right by. "Doesn't she know anything?" Terry asked from behind the plate.

Breezy turned to glare at Terry. It was all right if *she* criticized the players, because it was *her* team. But Terry wasn't the coach. "C.J., you've got to cover the bag!" Breezy called out.

Crystal moved over, until she was on top of the base. Terry laughed. Breezy ignored her and jogged out to first. "C.J., you've got to give the batter room to run through. Stand out here," Breezy explained as she moved a few feet to the left, away from the base. "When the ball comes your way, stretch to catch it, trying to keep one foot on or near the base." Breezy extended her foot and leaned toward the pitcher. "See?"

Crystal nodded slowly. "O.K., I think I've got it. I'm going to read up on first base tonight."

"Good." Breezy nodded, and patted her on the back. As she jogged back to home plate, she thought that no matter how weird it seemed to her that Crystal was learning baseball from a book, in a warped way she had to admit that it did kind of make sense.

Breezy picked up the bat and tapped a grounder out to Andrea at third. It rolled right between her legs. Betsy, in the outfield, didn't even move to come in for the ball. "Andy, get your glove on the ground!" Breezy yelled out. "Bets, you've got to back her up! If she misses it, you have to get it!"

Betsy shrugged her shoulders in leftfield and slowly walked toward the ball. Kim raced behind Andrea and got to it first. She threw it to Crystal, who was in the right spot, but dropped the ball when it got to her.

"Close your glove around the ball, C.J.!" Breezy yelled. Crystal nodded, and picked up the ball. She threw it to Terry. The ball hit the dirt a few feet to the right of home plate, about 10 feet away from where Terry was waiting for it. Obviously, Breezy thought, Crystal hadn't gotten to the "how-to-throw" chapter yet. "Great team, Breezy," Terry said sarcastically. "We're going to be laughed off the field at this rate."

"Hey, you don't have to be here, DiSunno," Breezy replied angrily.

"You're right," Terry agreed, handing the ball back to Breezy. "I'm just glad I didn't quit R & R Hardware yet."

"You can't be on two teams at once!" Breezy shouted. She couldn't understand why things weren't working out the way they were supposed to. "We'll get disqualified from the league if you do, Terry!"

"Don't worry about it," Terry said angrily. "I'm leaving!" She stomped over to her bag and started throwing her catching equipment into it.

"You're worse than Lindsay and Joey!" Breezy screamed back. "We don't need you!"

"Fine!" Terry yelled. "Don't call me when you lose every game!" She slung her bag over her shoulder and grabbed her sneakers. Without even changing out of her cleats she started stomping away. "You're just a bunch of amateurs anyway!" she screamed over her shoulder.

Breezy watched Terry walk away and then turned back to her team. She took a deep breath to calm herself. Kim started walking in from shortstop. Breezy motioned her back. They had to get this practice moving. Breezy tapped the ball between first and second. Neither Crystal nor Julie moved, and the ball rolled out to rightfield. Breezy sighed and dropped her bat. Terry was right. They *were* a bunch of amateurs. How in the world would she ever be able to pull this team together in time?

6

"I'm exhausted!" Kim moaned the next day. She flopped on top of Breezy's bed, which was unmade as usual. "What are we going to do?"

For once Breezy didn't have an answer. The two girls had spent all afternoon unsuccessfully combing Hampstead for a sponsor for their team.

"I can't believe every single one of them said no," Kim continued. She picked up a tennis ball from the floor and started tossing it in the air. "We're never going to find a sponsor in time."

"What time is the sponsor meeting?" Breezy asked, knocking a pile of sweats and T-shirts from her chair and sitting down. She gazed up at the poster of Dwight Gooden above her desk.

"Seven o'clock. We've only got two more hours," Kim replied, throwing the football on the floor. She glanced at the clock radio on the bookcase below Breezy's rows of trophies. "Hey, when did you get that one?" she asked, pointing at a new trophy. It was the only one among the swimming, ice hockey, basketball, baseball and soccer trophies that wasn't covered with dust, so it had to be new.

"Oh, I got that last weekend at that swim meet in Bowie," Breezy replied, walking over to the bookcase. She picked up the baseball sitting next to it and tossed it from hand to hand. The baseball was one of her prized possessions. Roger "Rocket Man" Clemens, the Red Sox' ace pitcher, had autographed it at an exhibition game against the Orioles last month in Baltimore.

"We'll never get a sponsor in time," Breezy went on. "I didn't think it was going to be this hard." Breezy had her heart set on pitching in Emblem this year. But after so many no's, she really didn't have a clue how they were going to find a sponsor in time for the league meeting that night.

"I don't know what we're going to do, Kim," said Breezy slowly. "But," she continued with renewed determination, "we can't give up. We still have two hours left." No way was she going to quit now, Breezy thought. Not while there was time left. "Yeah," Kim agreed, "I guess you're right. But I've got to get home. I've got to put dinner in the oven." Kim's mother worked full-time as a bookkeeper. She got dinner ready every morning before she went to work, but someone had to put it in the oven, so the family could eat when she and Mr. Yardley got home. Since Kim was the oldest of six kids, she was the one in charge of dinner.

"Can't somebody else do it?" Breezy asked, a little annoyed. Kim was always rushing home. Finding a sponsor was really important. "Couldn't your brother Richard do it for once? Just call him."

"Breezy, you know he won't. He never does," Kim said, rebraiding one of her pigtails. She stood up when she was finished. "Listen, I've got to go, Breeze. I'm sorry, but you know how it is. Give me a call if anything happens."

"Yeah, right," Breezy said, sitting down on the edge of her bed. "Bye."

"Talk to you later," Kim said as she left the room.

After the door closed, Breezy laid back and stared up at the ceiling. Two hours. What was she going to do? She glanced over at her poster of Janet Evans, the swimmer who had won three gold medals at the 1988 Olympics in Seoul, South Korea. Breezy had met Janet at a swimming clinic last summer. Janet had given her the poster on the last day of the clinic. She wrote on the bottom of it: "To Breezy Hawk, a future gold-medal winner. See you in the pool—Janet."

"AMY!" her mother called from downstairs. Breezy didn't answer right away. Whatever her mother wanted would have to wait. She heard her mother's footsteps coming up the stairs. "Amy," her mother said again, banging on her door. "Are you in there? Didn't you hear me?"

Breezy sighed and rolled over. "What do you want,

Mom?" she asked impatiently.

Mrs. Hawk opened the door and stepped inside. She frowned as she looked around the cluttered room. "When was the last time you cleaned this room, Amy?" she asked. "Didn't we talk about you making your bed?"

"Mom," Breezy said, sitting up. "*You* talked about making the bed. I just listened. Besides, what's the point? Why make the bed if you're just going to sleep in it in a few hours anyway?"

Breezy's mother sighed. "You're impossible, Amy. You're worse than your brothers."

Breezy shook her head. She had heard this so many times before. "I know, I know," she agreed impatiently.

"Oh, right," her mother replied. "I knew I came up here for something. Your Aunt June just called. Eddie has a big test or something tomorrow so he couldn't make it in to work. So she's stuck over at the diner. And Jazz is at the beauty parlor. Aunt June forgot to give her a check to pay for her haircut."

Breezy groaned. "So?" she asked. "What does that have to do with me?" She had a pretty good idea, but she decided to play dumb instead. Maybe her mother wouldn't say what she thought she was going to say, and she didn't want to put any ideas in her head.

"So, I need you to run a check over to Jazz at the Pink Parrot," her mother explained.

Breezy groaned again. Trust Jazz to get her hair cut at a place with a name like the Pink Parrot. Her cousin was such a ditz sometimes. "Mom, I don't have time to get Jazz out of another mess. You know I have to get a sponsor by seven." Her mother only had to give her one look, though, before she started putting on her high tops. "All right, all right," Breezy muttered. "I'll go. Jazz would forget her head if it wasn't attached."

"Yes, well . . ." Mrs. Hawk began philosophically, letting her voice trail off. "I'll go write the check." She walked out of the room, shaking her head one last time as she looked from the unmade bed to the cluttered floor to the dresser with clothes spilling out of it.

It would be all Jazz's fault if they didn't get a sponsor, Breezy fumed, knotting her sneakers tightly. She grabbed her sweatshirt and ran out of the room. She stopped in the kitchen to pick up the check and then zipped out the back door.

Biking furiously down Main Street, Breezy felt herself becoming more and more angry. Trust Jazz to pull something like this—at the worst possible time. Breezy was so angry at Jazz that she almost flew past the Pink Parrot Beauty Salon. Squeezing the brakes hard, she skidded to a stop in front of a two-story pink stucco building.

Breezy parked her bike out front and eyed the building warily. She didn't know how many times she had been past this building, but she had never been inside it before. Why in the world anybody would go to a beauty parlor to get a haircut was totally beyond Breezy. Her mother always cut her hair. She did Kim's, too. It figured someone as silly and vain and boy-crazy as Jazz would go to a place like this.

Pushing open the door, Breezy almost gagged at the smell of hairspray and nail polish in the air. "Yuck!" she said, wrinkling her nose. She walked over to the reception desk, but no one was there. Breezy tapped her foot impatiently—she did not have time for this.

"Be right with you, hon," a woman called out. Breezy looked around, but it was hard to tell who had spoken. There were four chairs positioned in front of huge mirrors near where she was standing—two on each side. A woman sat in the front seat on the right, covered with a huge flowered smock. One of the people who worked there was standing behind her putting what looked like tinfoil on the ends of her hair. Breezy had no idea what that was all about. She also had no clue whether the person behind the chair was a man or a woman. The person had really, really short bright red hair and was wearing a black shirt, black jeans and black cowboy boots. Breezy shook her head in confusion. Really weird.

Another woman was sitting with pink curlers on her head, surrounded by strange-looking red lights on stands. Every available space in the shop was covered with bottles and jars of unusually colored liquids. Breezy felt as if she was in a mad scientist's lab or something. The smell of chemicals was making her eyes water.

"*Caramba!*" a voice suddenly squawked from behind the desk, startling Breezy. She stood on her tiptoes to try

54

and see who was talking, but she couldn't see anyone.

"Hey, *chica*," the voice continued. Breezy looked around. No one was paying any attention to her, though. Then she heard a loud squawk. Looking back, Breezy's eyes widened in surprise. A large green parrot had flown onto the desk. "*Qué pasa?*" the parrot asked her. Breezy couldn't help herself and she giggled. It was really too funny—a parrot that spoke Spanish. Breezy was taking introductory Spanish this year in school, so she knew what the parrot was saying.

"So, honey, I'm Ro. What can I do for you?" said a woman behind Breezy. Breezy turned around and gaped. The first thing she noticed was hair—major hair. Ro's brown hair must have been a good six inches above her head. Breezy wondered how she got her hair to stand up like that. She remembered reading something about the law of gravity in a science class a few months ago, and that hair definitely looked as if it was breaking the law.

"Well?" Ro persisted, snapping her gum.

Breezy opened her mouth to say something, but nothing came out. She had thought the man, or woman, with red hair was something, but this woman was . . . she didn't know what. Ro was wearing a cropped black turtleneck, an extremely tight white mini-skirt, white lace stockings and black-and-white cowboy boots. And if the rest of her didn't look wild enough, Ro was wearing bright red lipstick.

"Don't worry, I can work with anything," the woman continued. Before Breezy could stop her, Ro reached over and pulled the rubber band out of Breezy's ponytail.

"Ouch!" Breezy exclaimed, staring at the woman's inch-long fingernails. They were painted the same color red as her lips.

"Well, it's not terrible. How much is going to go?" Ro asked, running her fingers through Breezy's dark blonde hair.

Breezy jerked her head back. "None of it!" she replied firmly. "You're not touching a hair on my head."

"Easy," Ro said, stepping back and holding her hands up. Her big silver hoop earrings swayed as she moved. Breezy thought they looked big enough to be bracelets.

"I'm looking for my cousin," Breezy snapped, grabbing her rubber band back. "Jazz Jaffe." She pulled her hair back into a tight ponytail. The last thing she wanted was for this wacked out woman to lay a finger on her hair.

"Jazz is under a dryer," Ro said, pointing to the back of the parlor. "She's almost done."

Breezy walked quickly over to the row of dryers. Jazz was sitting under the last one, flipping through a magazine. "Jazz!" Breezy called. Her cousin didn't look up. "*JAZZ!*" Breezy yelled a little more loudly. No response. Typical, Breezy thought. Even when Jazz was there, she wasn't really there. Finally, Breezy banged on the hood of the dryer. Jazz jumped in her seat and looked up, her blue eyes opened wide. She smiled when she saw Breezy. Reaching around, she turned the dryer off.

"What are you doing here, Breezy?" Jazz asked. Her long, honey blonde hair was all wound up in curlers. She patted the top of her head to see if her hair was dry.

Breezy rolled her eyes. "You forgot to bring a check to pay for this," she said, shaking her head at the thought of someone paying to get a haircut. She dropped the check onto Jazz's blue denim mini-skirt.

"I did?" Jazz asked, picking up the check in surprise. She looked at it, "There's no amount written here," she said, pointing to it.

Breezy sighed. How her cousin functioned was beyond her. "Jazz, you've got to fill it in yourself. My mother had no idea how much this was going to cost. Just remember the amount, O.K.?"

Jazz nodded and put the check in the pocket of the short white jacket she was wearing over a red tank top.

"I'm outta here," Breezy said, turning to go. "I've got no time!"

"Why are you in such a hurry?" Jazz asked. "Why don't you get your hair done, too? I'm sure your mother wouldn't mind. It would be fun."

Breezy just snorted and kept walking.

"Hey!" Ro called out just as Breezy reached the front door. Ro was standing near the back of the shop checking on Jazz's hair. She motioned Breezy back.

"What?" Breezy asked, impatiently turning around.

"I already said I didn't want my hair done."

Ro laughed. "I got the message. Nice J.R. Richard jersey you're wearing."

Breezy looked down at her Houston Astros shirt. She thought J.R. Richard had been a really good pitcher when he played in the 1970s. She wondered how in the world Ro would know who he was. He hadn't played for about ten years, and he wasn't even that well-known when he was pitching. The jersey was one of her favorite shirts.

"Too bad about that stroke that ended his career in 1980, huh?" Ro asked, but then went on before Breezy could answer. "With a hundred mile-per-hour fastball and a career 3.15 ERA over 10 years, he could have been one of the greats, if he hadn't had to quit."

"It was too bad his comeback didn't work out," Breezy added, getting into the discussion. Not too many people shared her addiction to baseball stats. Here was someone who truly appreciated the numbers. But a hairdresser? Breezy thought that she certainly didn't look the part of an avid baseball fan. Or a fan of any sport for that matter.

"Ro!" Jazz interrupted them. "Am I done yet?"

"Hold on a sec," Ro answered, studying Breezy. "How do you know about that? You couldn't have been more than two years old."

"How do you know so much about baseball?" Breezy countered, ignoring Ro's question.

"My father played for the New York Yankees Triple

58

A team in Richmond," Ro explained.

"Your *father* played minor league baseball?" Breezy asked. She was impressed. Maybe there was more to this Ro than hair.

"Yeah, he even played in the bigs for two whole weeks," Ro continued proudly. "But then one of his knees blew and he had to give it up. My brother plays Single A at Frederick now. He's only 18."

Ro's brother was on the Baltimore Orioles minor league team? That was incredible. "You're kidding?" Breezy asked in disbelief. She had never known anyone who had actually played professional baseball before. She couldn't imagine playing baseball as a job. That would be great.

"Ro!" Jazz interrupted again. "Am I done yet?" she repeated. "Breezy, let her check me. I thought you had to go somewhere, anyway."

"Breezy?" Ro asked in surprise, walking back to touch Jazz's hair. "One more minute," she said to Jazz and turned back to Breezy. "That name sounds familiar. Where do I know you from?"

"You don't," Breezy replied. She had very definitely never met this woman before. And she had never been in the Pink Parrot Beauty Salon either.

"Breezy Hawk!" Ro suddenly shouted. "Now I know who you are. I cut Jim Stepanic's hair a half hour ago. You know, the guy from the auto parts store. He told me all about you. You're trying to find a sponsor for your team, aren't you?"

Breezy frowned. "That guy was one of the worst," she admitted. He had practically split his side laughing when she and Kim had told him about an all-*girls* baseball team. Breezy couldn't understand what the big deal was anyway.

"So did you get one?" Ro asked, flipping Jazz's dryer back on. Her boots clacked on the linoleum as she walked over to Breezy. "What's the story?"

"There is no story," Breezy replied.

"Why not?" Ro asked, curious. "You mean you don't have a sponsor yet?"

"Right," Breezy replied. "But I'm going to that meeting anyway. They can't keep my team out of the league." Breezy got angry all over again just thinking about how Mr. Egan, the head of Emblem, had looked so smug when he told her she had to have a sponsor in order to have a team, adding that he doubted she'd be able to find one. And to top it all off, he had called her "doll" and "sweetie" twice. That ticked her off almost more than anything else.

Ro sat down in an empty chair and crossed her legs, swinging one cowboy boot back and forth. "There's a league meeting tonight?" Ro asked with a crack of her gum.

"Yeah, in about half an hour," Breezy said, sitting down next to Ro. "They told me I had to have a sponsor by tonight in order to play."

"You don't have one?" Ro asked thoughtfully. Breezy nodded. Ro studied her intently for a moment. "Well, what if I was your sponsor?"

Breezy's mouth dropped open. "What?"

"Yeah, the Pink Parrot will be your sponsor!" Ro repeated, jumping up in excitement.

"Great!" Breezy exclaimed.

"We better get going if we're going to make that meeting on time," Ro said.

"RO!" Jazz's voice called from the back. "Am I done yet?"

"Oh, no!" Ro exclaimed. "I forgot all about you," she said and laughed. She dashed back and shut off the dryer. "You're fine. I've got to go, but Marcel will comb you out."

"Where are you going, Ro?" Jazz asked, standing up.

"We're going to the Emblem meeting," Breezy cut in. "Ro's going to be my baseball team's sponsor."

"We better get going," Ro said, practically dragging Breezy out of the shop.

Breezy turned and gave Jazz a little wave on her way out. Ro would sponsor them and Breezy would coach. Ro might not be Breezy's idea of the ideal sponsor, but still. Now her team would finally be able to really show Joey Carpenter and his father that girls could play baseball as well as boys—better even!

61

7

"You should have seen Coach Carpenter's face last night," Breezy said to Kim the next afternoon. "He practically swallowed his cigar when he saw me—*and* Ro." Breezy sat down and untied her sneakers. She pulled her cleats out of her gym bag and shoved her feet into them. Tightening the laces, she looked up at Kim and grinned. "Carpenter didn't seem too happy when he found out I was going to pitch in Emblem after all."

"I wish I could have been there!" Kim exclaimed, plopping down next to Breezy on the grass. Breezy and Kim were at Fireman's Field waiting for everyone else to show up for practice. "So what happened? I want details," Kim asked.

"Well, I told you that everyone just stopped talking when Ro and I walked in," Breezy said. She stood up and pulled her baseball cap down on her head. "My muscles are *so* tight!" she continued, stretching her legs.

Breezy had been so excited after she came back from the meeting the night before that she hadn't been able to sit still. She had driven her family crazy until her brother Tom dragged her out for a two-mile run. But she probably hadn't stretched enough afterward and now her legs were tight.

"Then what happened?" Kim asked, trying to get Breezy back on the topic. "You never finish a story!"

"I do, too," Breezy shot back. "My legs are killing me!" She stretched again and groaned.

"Breezy!" Kim yelled impatiently. "What happened after that?"

Breezy laughed. Sometimes she just liked to drive Kim crazy. She had every intention of telling Kim what had happened at the Emblem meeting, but she wanted her best friend to get a little worked up first. "Well . . ." she began, pausing dramatically.

Kim threw her glove at Breezy, who ducked, and the glove plunked down somewhere on the grass behind her. "Then Ro said she wanted to register a new team— the Pink Parrots. Mr. Egan tried to talk her out of it. He said there couldn't possibly be any such thing as an all-girls baseball team. Then Carpenter actually called her a 'little lady,'" Breezy continued, as she rummaged for a baseball in her bag.

Kim giggled. "A little lady? What'd Ro say?"

"Ro walked right up to him and told him that she hoped she wouldn't have to take this matter to Emblem's Board of Directors," Breezy replied with a smile at the memory. "Ro said that it would be a really messy court case, all over the newspapers and stuff . . . ."

"She didn't!" Kim exclaimed, snickering. "Coach Carpenter must have really loved that!"

"You should have been there! It was wild," Breezy replied, throwing the ball into her glove. "He was so upset that he kept spitting out little pieces of cigar all over the place. I just wish Joey had been there. That would have been great!"

"No kidding," Kim agreed. "Hey, what time did you tell everyone to get here anyway?"

Breezy looked at her watch. "They should be here by now," she admitted. The rest of the team had better show up now that they had a sponsor. "Anyway," she continued, "what Ro said about taking the matter before the Board must have really scared Mr. Egan because he rushed to fill out all the papers to sign up the Pink Parrots. I wanted to laugh so much. Hey, don't forget to stretch, Kim."

Kim sat down and pulled her legs out into a split, at least as far as she could go. She leaned down over her right leg, moaning a little. "I hate stretching!"

"And then Mr. Egan said that he had to have a roster by tomorrow. We still need two more players. And he had to make up new team schedules for everyone and Ro would get ours today," Breezy said, reaching her arms up over her head. She shifted her weight from one foot to the other and back again. "I can't wait to see who we'll play this weekend. I hope it's Mitchell Lumber!"

"Wouldn't that be great!" Kim agreed. "Of course, we're going to have to practice a lot, huh?"

Breezy stopped stretching—Kim was right. What was she thinking? Almost no one on the Pink Parrots knew how to play. At least not yet. And they couldn't play Mitchell Lumber until they could win. Nothing would be worse than losing and having to face Joey. He would never let them forget it. And the Pink Parrots really stank now. They were going to have to practice—*a lot.*

"Hi, guys," Crystal greeted them, setting her bag on the grass. "Sorry I'm late. I was in the library." She held up a new baseball book—*How to Hit Any Pitch.*

"Hey, C.J.," Breezy said, grabbing the book. "Let me see that." She leafed through it quickly. Breezy had never seen a "how-to" book on baseball before Crystal started carting them all over the place. Crystal could probably write one someday, Breezy figured. Still, Breezy was glad that Crystal was trying so hard to learn the game.

"We're stretching," Kim explained to Crystal, reaching over to grab her right foot as she got in a semi-split position. "It's important to warm up before playing ball."

Breezy nodded her head in agreement. It was bad enough that no one knew how to play. The last thing the Pink Parrots needed was a bunch of players with pulled muscles. Rule Number One would be everyone has to stretch, Breezy decided.

"We also stretch out in dancing," Crystal replied. "I

probably can use the same stretches for this, right?"

"Sure, why not?" Breezy answered with a shrug. She had no idea how a dancer stretched, but she figured stretching was stretching.

Crystal kicked her right leg straight up in front of her, so that her knee was practically next to her ear. Then, she did the same with her left leg. "Yikes!" Breezy exclaimed, staring at Crystal. "Doesn't that hurt?"

"Even your toes are pointed!" Kim added, enviously. "How do you do that?" She stood up next to Crystal.

Crystal shrugged. "I don't know," she replied. "Dancing, I guess."

"Maybe I should take up dancing," Kim said. "I can barely touch my toes." She bent over and only reached midway down her shins.

"It takes practice," Crystal said. "Just keep working on it."

"Hey, C.J.!" Breezy suddenly exclaimed. "I got a sponsor last night—just in the nick of time, too."

"Really?" Crystal asked excitedly. "Who is it? And what's the name of our team going to be?"

"Rose Ann DiMona is our sponsor. Well actually, it's her beauty shop, the Pink Parrot, that's the sponsor," Breezy replied.

"Why is it called the Pink Parrot anyway?" Kim asked, snatching the ball from Breezy's glove. They started throwing it back and forth between them.

"Oh, I forgot to tell you about that!" Breezy said,

raising her voice. She threw the ball back at Kim. "Well, you know the beauty shop is in that building that's all pink."

Kim giggled. "Oh, yeah," she replied.

"Where is this place?" Crystal asked.

Breezy had forgotten that Crystal hadn't lived in Hampstead for long. "Well, you know where the auto parts store is, don't you?"

Crystal shook her head.

"How about the library?" Breezy asked, trying again. "You *must* know where that is, don't you C.J.?"

"You know I do," she replied, laughing.

"Well, about four buildings down Main Street, on the other side, there's this pink building." Breezy couldn't imagine how anyone could miss it. Crystal must have seen it at least once, even though she had her nose in a book all the time. The place *was* pink after all.

"A pink building?" Crystal asked, a little surprised. "A pink building is our sponsor?"

"Sort of," Breezy admitted. "Actually, it's a beauty parlor *inside* the pink building. It's a little embarrassing. But at least we're registered." She had been trying all last night to think of a way to get out of wearing the name "Pink Parrot" on their baseball jerseys. Every other team in the league had its sponsor's name on its jerseys. Breezy hoped that maybe there wasn't actually a rule that you *had* to.

"But why Pink *Parrot*?" Crystal asked, putting on a

brand new baseball glove.

"You're going to have to break that glove in, C.J.," Breezy said as she walked over to Crystal. "Let me see it."

Crystal pulled her glove off and handed it to Breezy. Breezy took hers off and put Crystal's on. "You have to oil this, you know."

"Oh, yeah," Crystal replied. "I read about that last night. Don't you have to put a baseball inside and leave it like that overnight or something? I wanted to ask you about that."

Breezy looked at her in surprise. Those books really *were* teaching Crystal about baseball. "Yeah," she replied. "And don't forget to tie some string around your glove to keep it tight around the ball."

"I always put mine under my mattress to loosen it up," Kim added helpfully, as she walked over to them. "Breezy, you never answered the question. Why parrot?" she asked.

"Get this," Breezy began. "Ro's actually got this parrot in her shop. It scared me to death when I was there last night. The parrot flies all over the place. I mean, it's not in a cage or anything. And it talks to you—in Spanish!"

"What?" Kim asked, astonished. "You're joking. A real parrot? That's wild!"

"Seriously," Breezy replied. "It kept saying '*caramba*' and stuff."

"And Ro is Rose Ann DiMona?" Crystal asked, taking her glove back from Breezy.

"Right," Breezy replied. "And everyone calls her Ro."

"Ro sounds kind of interesting," Kim commented. "I mean she sure doesn't sound like your typical adult."

"All right! We're good to go!" Breezy suddenly exclaimed as she saw some of the team start straggling slowly toward them across the field.

8

After the other girls had finally made it out to where Breezy, Kim and Crystal were, they just stood there. "C.J.'s going to lead you all in stretching," Breezy said briskly. "Everyone's got to warm up first."

Crystal didn't look as if she wanted to lead anything, but Breezy gave her a gentle push forward. "Stand in front of everyone," she instructed. "You don't have to say anything if you don't want to. Just stretch." Crystal looked a little uncertain, but Breezy grinned and winked at her. Then Crystal slowly smiled and everyone, following her lead, started stretching.

When they were finished, Breezy handed out a couple of balls. "Everyone pair up and just start tossing the ball back and forth. Get your arms loose," she instructed. "Oh, no!" she exclaimed suddenly, catching sight of her cousin, Jazz, walking across the field.

"Bree-zy!" Jazz called, waving at her and strolling slowly toward the team. Breezy shook her head in disgust. What was her cousin doing here?

"Bree-zy!" Jazz called again, coming closer.

"Why are you here?" Breezy asked. She didn't have time for any of Jazz's nonsense.

Jazz pouted for a minute. "Mom told me I had to join your team. Your mother told me where you were, so here I am."

Breezy groaned. Her Aunt June was always forcing Jazz to hang out with her. And Breezy's mother was always forcing her to be nice to her cousin. Mrs. Hawk and Mrs. Jaffe thought it would be good for Jazz to get away from the mall and think about something else besides boys.

"It's so hot out here, can't we sit in the shade?" Jazz asked. The afternoon sun was still bright and there were no trees at all on the field.

Breezy sighed. "Jazz, you can sit in the shade if you want to, but we've got to practice," she replied. Breezy shook her head again. Her cousin was definitely not dressed to play baseball anyway. Jazz had on pale yellow overall shorts with a white tank top—and very clean white Keds. Her fingernails were painted white. "Why don't you go sit over there?" Breezy suggested, pointing at the bleachers.

"Is everyone else going to sit down, too?" Jazz asked, puzzled. She smoothed back her already smooth honey blonde ponytail. Breezy couldn't believe it—she even had a matching pale yellow scrunchie in her hair. Breezy didn't even answer her. "Well, I don't want to be the only one sitting down. If everyone else is playing then I want to, too," Jazz whined.

Breezy thought her cousin was such a baby sometimes. She always had to get her way. Breezy had never understood why she was so popular, but boys were always falling all over Jazz.

"Tough," Breezy said. "Besides, you don't know the first thing about baseball."

Jazz stuck out her lower lip. "I don't want to sit down. You can't make me," she insisted, tugging on her overall strap and staring at Breezy, her blue eyes wide.

Breezy sighed again. Why was Jazz such a pain about everything?

"Ro will tell you to let me play, Breezy," Jazz continued, looking over her cousin's shoulder. "Here she comes now," she announced with a smile.

Breezy spun around. What was Ro doing here? This team needed every possible moment of practice. They didn't have time to meet with their sponsor.

"What's going on?" Ro called to Breezy.

Breezy's mouth opened in astonishment. She thought Ro had looked a little wild the night before with her mini-skirt and all, but this was . . . this was . . . Breezy couldn't even think of words to describe it. Ro's hair was even bigger today. Breezy thought she would probably topple over in a strong wind. Ro was wearing bright pink high-top Reeboks, thick fuschia socks, leopard-print leggings and a fuschia cut-up sweatshirt over a yellow tank top. Her nails were fluorescent pink today and she was carrying a large radio and a pink duffle bag.

"Well, don't just stand there," Ro said to Breezy. "Take this bag."

Breezy walked over to Ro and took the bag.

"So, this is my team?" Ro commented as she looked around. "There are only eight girls here." Ro snapped her gum and blew a big bubble, studying them.

"Well . . ." Breezy began defensively. But wait a minute, she thought. This was *her* team—it just happened to be named after Ro's beauty parlor. "There's another one coming," Breezy finally said, as she nudged Kim, signaling her not to say anything.

"O.K.," Ro answered, setting the radio up on the first step of the bleachers. She opened her bag and pulled out a stack of tapes. "But if the other person doesn't show up soon, we'll have to start without her."

"We started already," Kim added. She flung both her braids over her shoulders and stared at Ro.

"That's good," Ro said. "But now that I'm here we can really get going."

Breezy was getting worried. She couldn't understand what difference Ro thought it made if she was there or not.

"I'm sorry I'm a little late," Ro continued. "But Miss Forrester—you know the woman who works in the post office—came in and needed to get her hair set before her date tonight. She said it was a real emergency. It was, too!

Anyway, now I'm here and we can start practice," she finished.

"We *were* practicing," Breezy answered a little defiantly. She pounded her glove. "We were throwing the ball around."

"Yeah, I saw you," Ro said, pulling her hair up into a high ponytail on top of her head. She put a bright pink scrunchie around it. "But we've got to get into condition before we work on skills. My brother always tells me that. You know, like spring training."

"What are you talking about?" Breezy demanded. "We've got a game coming up this weekend." They didn't have time for "conditioning." Kim and Sarah were the only other Pink Parrots who even knew how to throw a baseball.

"I know," Ro agreed. "But you've got to be in shape to play baseball. So are you girls ready?"

Ready for what, Breezy wondered. She opened her mouth to ask Ro, but Ro cut her off. "Don't worry, Breezy. We'll get to skills, too." Ro turned around and started to fiddle with her radio. "I'm sure I'll be different from your other coaches, but I promise you, this is going to be great." Ro clapped her hands excitedly.

"But you're just the sponsor!" Breezy burst out. "*I'm* the coach."

"Breezy, you're only twelve," Ro said with a smile.

"So what?" Breezy snapped back.

"Well, Mr. Egan gave me a rulebook last night at the

meeting. I read it after I got home, and it said that coaches have to be over eighteen," Ro said. "I am *definitely* over eighteen." She paused and bent down to rummage through her bag again. "So, we better get going. Let's rock and roll!"

Breezy sputtered, and turned around. Kim just shrugged at her helplessly, and the rest of the team looked from Breezy to Ro and back again. Breezy had never heard of that stupid rule about coaches having to be so old. Anyway, her team couldn't be coached by a hairdresser! They'd be laughed right out of Emblem!

"Come on, girls!" Ro called. She put a tape in the radio. "Let's line up." Jazz was the only one who moved. She jumped right in front of Ro and smiled. Breezy just stood where she was, waiting to see what Ro was going to pull next.

Ro swung around and saw that her team still hadn't moved. "Hey!" she called. "You guys are like a bunch of lumps!" She moved to the front of the line. "I want everyone to call out their names for me, starting with Jazz!" Everyone introduced themselves. Then Ro started to repeat all the names, frowning in concentration and pointing—Jazz, Breezy, Kim, Crystal, Julie, Betsy, Sarah, Andrea. Breezy was impressed—she got every single name right.

Then, suddenly, Technotronics' song "Pump Up the Jam!" came blaring out of the speakers.

"This is my favorite song!" Julie squealed and jumped

in line next to Jazz. Before Breezy could move a muscle, the rest of the Pink Parrots had fallen into line as well. Kim looked back at Breezy and shrugged.

Breezy jammed her hat down harder on her head. They weren't supposed to be listening to music during practice. They should be hitting, or fielding or something. Breezy decided to play along for a while until Ro got the message and gave up. Breezy did not doubt for a single second that Ro would never cut it—she couldn't possibly know the first thing about coaching.

"All right, girls!" Ro called, standing in front of them. "Time to twist! Twist your hips to the left and arms to the right, and then switch!" Ro started twisting back and forth. Breezy looked down the line of girls. Her cousin was flinging her arms back and forth wildly. She looked ridiculous. And to make matters worse, everyone else was twisting away—even Kim. "Swing those hips, girls! Really feel the beat!"

Breezy shrugged and started twisting. It wasn't baseball, but she had to admit that at least it was exercise.

"Arms higher, Julie!" Ro sang out, moving among the girls, correcting their movements as she went. "Now, bend your knees!" Ro called, moving back to the face the team. "And twist all the way down to the ground!"

Breezy started twisting lower and lower. She couldn't believe it—this was not as easy as it sounded. Her quadricep muscles in the front of her thighs were really starting to burn.

"Back up!" Ro called, slowly twisting until she was standing up again. "Good!" she said, complimenting them when all the Pink Parrots were standing. "Now, put your hands on the ground a few feet in front of you. And straighten your legs out in back of you, almost like you were doing push-ups."

Everyone fell forward. Breezy groaned. This really hurt the backs of her legs.

"Raise your heels and lower them," Ro continued, assuming the same position. "Feel the burn in your calves?"

"O.K., now slowly stand up, girls!" Ro called, after a few minutes. She stood up, and looked beyond the team for a moment. "Oh, you finally made it!" she exclaimed, waving someone forward.

Breezy turned around and saw Terry, holding a bat behind her shoulders, walking slowly across the field toward the team. Her baseball hat was on backwards, and she was wearing old, ratty black sweatpants and a big white T-shirt that had the word "Attitude" printed across the front. Her black high tops were untied and her cleats were hanging over the end of her bat. Breezy thought she had seen the end of Terry after their last practice.

"Good," Ro said, motioning Terry into the line next to Breezy. "Now, we're all here. What's your name?"

Terry walked over to stand next to Breezy and glared at her. Then she turned toward Ro. "Terry. Terry Di-

Sunno," she growled.

"Hi, Terry. I'm Ro," Ro said and smiled. "Get into line. We're warming up."

Breezy stared back at Terry. "What are you doing here?" Breezy hissed under her breath, as Ro started them running in place. "I thought you didn't want to play with a bunch of amateurs."

"I changed my mind," Terry shot back, out of breath already.

"Yeah, right," Andrea cut in, panting. "I heard R & R Hardware didn't want you back because someone told them you were playing on our team."

"Do you want me on your team or not?" Terry demanded. "I don't have to stay, you know."

"Of course we do, Terry," Kim called out. "We're glad you came back."

Breezy frowned. She was kind of glad Terry had shown up—she was a great catcher after all. But Breezy wasn't about to let her know that. Not after the way she'd just walked out on them last time. But Terry also happened to be the only real slugger they had, so her showing up was probably all for the best.

"Lift your knees higher!" Ro shouted. Everyone on the team started breathing hard then. Ro wasn't letting them take a break. The first song ended and "Stomp!" by K-Yse came on. "Now, lift your heels!" Ro called out. "Hit your butts with your heels!"

After a few minutes of this, Breezy thought her legs

were going to collapse. The backs of them were actually burning. This was not easy. "All right, team, now we're ready to go," Ro finally said. Breezy tried to catch her breath and thought, ready to go where? Ro turned off the radio and went to the front of the line. "All right, guys, let's move out!"

Ro started jogging off the field. The girls just kept running in place. Why were they leaving the field in the first place? They were supposed to be practicing, not running around.

"Come on!" Ro called, waving the girls to follow her. Jazz led the way. She wasn't moving very fast, though. The rest of the team straggled after her. Breezy took a deep breath.

Kim fell into step beside Breezy. "Where are we going?" she asked.

Breezy shrugged. "I don't know," she replied with a frown. "But I'm sick of running and I want to play ball already."

"If you're getting tired, everyone else must be dead," Kim teased her friend, giggling. "I'm beat."

Ro zipped out of the park, and turned down Main Street toward downtown Hampstead. The pack of girls followed after her.

Ro's wacky outfit turned heads the whole way into town. Breezy was a little embarrassed, especially when passing cars honked at them. Ro kept right on moving, though. She acted as if she didn't even notice.

Finally, when they got to the library courtyard, Ro slowed down. Everyone stopped and bent over, panting. "Don't stop! Run in place!" she called out. Ro bounded to the center of the courtyard. "Now, 'Groucho Walk'!" she directed.

The team stopped and looked at each other, puzzled. Breezy had no idea what a "Groucho Walk" was. Ro crouched down a little, and started walking around in circles really fast. She pretended that she had a cigar and shook one hand up and down near her mouth. "Come on, girls! What are you waiting for?"

Jazz imitated Ro first, giggling the whole time. "Bend your knees a little more, Jazz," Ro instructed. "When you feel pain in your quads, you're doing it right. Come on, you guys!" Ro called to the rest of them. "This is great for your legs!"

Terry raised her eyebrows at Breezy. Breezy frowned, but started Groucho Walking. Terry followed. "I feel ridiculous," Terry muttered behind Breezy. Breezy grunted in agreement. Ro was right. It did hurt—a lot. But Breezy knew that if it hurt, the Groucho Walk must be doing some good.

Soon the whole team was Groucho Walking all over the courtyard. The library doors opened and about 20 mothers and their children spilled out. Story hour had just ended. They all stopped and stared at the Pink Parrots. Breezy bent her knees more and walked even faster. She glanced over at Kim, who was cracking up. In fact, it seemed as if the whole team was giggling. It was hard to keep up, but there was something about the Groucho Walk that made all the girls smile. Even Breezy couldn't stop herself from smiling. It was so silly looking.

"All right, enough!" Ro finally called out. Everyone stopped dead in their tracks. "Don't stop! Keep moving! Jog in place!"

The team let out a collective groan but started jogging. Breezy's quads hurt so much she could barely lift her feet. "Now, we're going to do Boings!" Ro sang out cheerfully.

Breezy felt like killing Ro. It was bad enough making the Pink Parrots do all these crazy, painful things in public, but to be happy about it on top of that was really bizarre.

"She's a maniac!" Terry exclaimed under her breath to Breezy. Terry looked as if she was going to pass out. She was sweating so much that it was dripping off her nose. Breezy nodded in agreement. Ro was crazy. What the heck was a Boing anyway? Ro bent down, leaned forward on her toes and put one hand on the ground. "Get into the 'Hut' position that football players use," she instructed the team. "Now Boing all over the place!"

Ro started bouncing up and down on her toes around the courtyard. The girls followed her example.

After a few minutes, Breezy thought she was going to keel over. She was exhausted. But Ro had them line up and Boing around the edge of the courtyard. Jazz did three Boings and collapsed on the pavement. Julie and Betsy didn't even make it halfway. Andrea, Terry and Sarah dropped out soon after that. Kim made it almost all the way, but fell over just short. Breezy couldn't believe that she and Crystal were the only ones other than Ro—the superhuman endurance machine—who actually made it all the way around. Breezy stood up and looked back. The Pink Parrots were lying everywhere, gasping. Ro, her ponytail bouncing as she jogged in place, was still smiling.

"O.K., girls, follow me!" she sang out as she started jogging out of the courtyard back onto Main Street. The Parrots groaned and struggled to their feet. They formed a feeble line behind Crystal and Breezy.

"Where are we going now?" Kim asked. Breezy shook her head without saying anything. She had a feeling she was going to have to conserve all her energy for whatever Ro had planned for them next. The only thing Coach Carpenter had ever made them do was jumping jacks, push-ups and sit-ups, and they were nothing compared to this stuff.

Ro was waiting for the team in front of the florist. She had stopped right by a parking meter. "Girls," she said, "we're going to work on muscle control now."

Muscle control? Breezy thought. Whatever it was, it sounded painful.

"I want you all to hop around five parking meters on one foot, then turn around and hop back on the other foot," Ro instructed them. She zig-zagged around the row of meters on her right foot, paused at the end, smiled and waved at the team, then zipped back on her left foot. Breezy couldn't believe it. Ro was hardly even breathing hard when she stopped.

"I'm not going to live through this," Terry said, moaning quietly. Breezy nodded her head. She didn't see how she was going to do it either. And she didn't know how she would get back to Fireman's Field and work on skills, too. It was going to be a really long afternoon. But she squared her shoulders and threw her chin forward. Stepping past all the other Pink Parrots, Breezy started hopping around the parking meters on her left foot. A hairdresser, wearing *pink* sneakers, was not going to get the best of her.

9

The first conscious thought Breezy had when she woke up on Saturday morning was that her whole body ached—especially her legs. The second was that the Pink Parrots were going to be playing their first game that day. The first practice with Ro two days ago had been a total killer. After they had finished hopping around all those parking meters, they had had to jog back to the field and Ro had then had them work on fielding and batting for another hour. Yesterday's practice had been more of the same. Breezy even had trouble lifting her arms to wash her hair in the shower on Friday. The practices were tough, but she didn't think the Pink Parrots were prepared yet to play an actual game. The majority of the players still couldn't catch the ball, and only she, Kim and Terry could throw with any kind of accuracy—or distance. Maybe if she stayed in bed the whole day, the game would never happen.

"Yo, Breezy, get moving!" Danny, Breezy's nine-year-old brother, called from the hallway outside her room.

Of course, Breezy was going to get up. She definitely wasn't the type to hide out in her bedroom and wait for something bad to go away. "Dad's got to drive me over to the park and he doesn't want to have to come back and get you an hour later!" Danny shouted.

Breezy moaned and rolled over. All her brothers were on baseball teams, too. Her parents usually went crazy every weekend trying to get everyone where they should be and catch at least part of each game along the way.

The door swung open and Danny burst in. "It's all over, Breeze," he warned. Breezy's only response was a groan. Her head was under her pillow so she didn't see her two older brothers, 15-year-old Russ and 16-year-old Tom, standing behind Danny. "That's it, you've had your chance to get your bod out of bed."

The boys all rushed the bed at once and sat on top of Breezy. "It's a Breezy-Sit!" Tom called out.

"Breezy-Sit, Breezy-Sit," Russ and Danny echoed.

"Get off me!" Breezy yelled, trying to squirm out from under them. "You guys are heavy!"

"Are you going to get up?" Danny asked.

"Yes!" Breezy yelled out, breathing heavily. Her brothers were not light. After what seemed like forever to Breezy, they finally got off of her. Then, Tom whipped the covers back. She yelped.

"Up and at 'em, Atom Ant!" he yelled. Atom Ant had been Breezy's favorite cartoon when she was little. For a while, she even thought she *was* Atom Ant. Her brothers had never let her forget it. In fact, they never let her forget anything.

Breezy rolled over and stood up, glaring at the three of them. Her hands were on her hips. They just grinned at her. "I'm up! Satisfied?"

"No," Danny retorted, scooping up her sweats and throwing them at her. "Get dressed, eat and get in the car. Then, I'll be satisfied."

Breezy stuck her tongue out at him, grabbed her bathrobe and ran for the bathroom. She thought brothers could be such a pain sometimes—especially three of them.

Twenty minutes later, she was dressed, fed and sitting in the car with her father, waiting for Danny. He, of course, was still eating breakfast. Typical, she thought.

Finally, they got over to the park. The Pink Parrots were playing Tony's Pizzeria on field number three, so Breezy headed over there to stretch and warm up. When she got there, the only person around was a man who was chalking the baselines. But within 20 minutes, almost every member of both teams had shown up and the stands were filling with people. Breezy led the Pink Parrots through some stretches and warmups.

"Where's Ro?" Crystal asked, five minutes before the game.

Breezy was pacing back and forth in front of the bench. She got nervous before every game and, in fact, every other sporting event she was ever in. She couldn't help it. No matter what, she always got major butterflies in her stomach. "I don't know," she answered, a little sharply.

Mr. Manuli, the coach of Tony's Pizzeria, had already been over to their dugout twice, asking where Ro was. He said that if she wasn't there within 15 minutes after the game was scheduled to begin, the Pink Parrots would have to forfeit. Breezy was fuming. They would *not* forfeit their first game, especially since she was the starting pitcher. Ro had better show up—and fast.

"And where's Jazz?" Kim asked. She grabbed Breezy's shoulders to keep her from pacing and made her sit down. "Be calm," she scolded. "You don't want to use up all your energy."

Breezy snorted. She should have known better than to count on Jazz for anything. Unfortunately, Jazz was the ninth player and they couldn't play without her. Even if Ro showed up soon, the rules said they'd have to forfeit if they were a player short.

Terry started buckling her pads. "Well, I probably should get ready just in case," she said to no one in particular. Breezy didn't think that Terry really looked like she was into the game. In fact, the only people who looked even halfway into playing were Kim and Crystal. Sarah was yawning with a half-asleep expression on her face. Betsy had finally bought a glove, but it hung limply from her hand as if the weight of it was too much for her to handle. And Julie and Andrea were playing *cards* at the far end of the dugout! Breezy shook her head. She guessed she should feel lucky they had showed up at all.

"Here comes Ro!" Kim suddenly exclaimed, jumping up and walking out of the dugout.

Breezy walked over to the edge and looked out. She couldn't help it, she gaped. Ro was striding purposefully toward them with her pink duffle bag hanging off one shoulder and a big mesh bag hanging off the other. Her hair was pulled into a high ponytail on top of her head and secured with a big, bright pink bow. She was wearing a pair of fuschia running tights, under a stretchy black mini-skirt. Her white T-shirt had "Pink Parrots" stenciled on it in hot pink letters, and she was wearing black-and-pink high-top sneakers. Breezy's mouth dropped open in surprise. Ro didn't even look remotely like a baseball coach. The other team was going to laugh them right off the field.

"Hi, girls!" Ro said, greeting the team. She brushed past Breezy and walked into the dugout. "Sorry I'm late. I completely forgot about the wedding party I had to do this morning."

Mr. Manuli walked over to the Pink Parrots. "You girls don't have much time left," he said, looking at his watch. His black hair was peppered with gray and he was wearing flip-up sunglasses, the kind that clipped onto the regular glasses. Breezy's father had them, too. "I wasn't at the meeting the other night," he grumbled, "but if I had been, I sure wouldn't have let a female team in, with a female coach!"

"It's nice to meet you anyway," Ro said. "My name's Rose Ann DiMona. Sorry I'm late."

Coach Manuli was very definitely at a loss for words. Breezy had to clamp her lips shut to keep from laughing. Coach Manuli flipped his sunglasses up and looked Ro up and down, very slowly. *"You're* the coach?" he finally said.

Ro just nodded with a smile, not at all bothered by Coach Manuli and his attitude.

"Well, let's get going, I guess," Coach Manuli finally said, flipping his glasses down again.

"Yeah," Ro agreed. "But I need a few minutes to go over my lineup."

"Sure," he called over his shoulder, shaking his head the whole way back to his team.

"So," Ro said, turning to the Pink Parrots and snapping her gum. "Everyone here?"

"Jazz isn't," Breezy answered shortly. She should've known Jazz wouldn't last.

Ro just nodded. "I'm sure she'll get here. Anyway, here's the lineup."

Breezy stopped listening after she heard she was pitching and batting first. She was getting a little worried about Jazz. If she didn't get there soon, there'd be no game.

"O.K.!" Ro exclaimed when she finished reading the roster. She clapped her hands together a few times. She dragged the mesh bag over to the bench and opened it. "I didn't have enough time to get the uniforms, but I got us all hats." The coach pulled out a few and started passing them around. When Ro got to her, Breezy couldn't help herself, she shrunk back as if the hat would bite her. The baseball hats were *pink*. Breezy couldn't believe it!

Just then, the umpire walked over to the fence in front of their dugout. "Time to take the field!" he called out, adjusting his black chest protector.

Breezy kicked the bench with her cleats. She was literally going to murder Jazz when she got her hands on her. She jammed her hot pink cap on her head and hoped that none of her family came to the game. She would hate for them to see her wearing this ridiculous pink hat.

"Oh, Jazz, here's your hat," Breezy heard Julie say behind her. She spun around and there was her cousin, all smiles. Not a hair was out of place, and she wasn't even breathing heavily. It was obvious to Breezy that Jazz hadn't been rushing to get to the game at all.

Breezy stalked up to Jazz, and put her face right next to her cousin's. "Where were you?" she asked through clenched teeth. Jazz obviously didn't know how close she was to death.

Jazz took a step back, her smile wavering a little. "But Breezy," she began. "You told me that we weren't up first, so I figured I could be a little late." Jazz looked confused.

Breezy shook her head. She must not have heard her right. Who did she think was going to be in the field when the other team was batting? Did she really think both teams didn't have to be there at the same time?

"Let's go, girls!" Ro called out, cutting Breezy off.

The rest of the Pink Parrots took the field, as Breezy jogged out to the pitcher's mound. She waited for Terry to amble over to the plate. Breezy couldn't believe the whole team's total lack of hustle.

Terry finally crouched behind the plate and Breezy put both feet on the rubber and leaned forward with the glove and ball in front of her. She got ready to rock back and start her windup, then realized that she and Terry hadn't worked out any signals at all. She motioned the catcher out to the mound.

"What?" Terry asked sharply when she got there. "Let's get going."

"Signals," Breezy shot back, popping a huge wad of bubblegum in her mouth.

Terry hit her helmet with her mitt. "Right," she said. "One finger, fastball; two, change-up. I'll pat my leg twice for inside corner and once for outside. Got it?"

Breezy had been nodding her head throughout Terry's instructions. Then she blew a giant bubble. "O.K.," she replied.

Turning away without another word, Terry walked back to home plate. Breezy starting throwing warmup pitches. After she'd grooved a few good ones in, the first batter started taking practice swings. The umpire signaled for all the balls on the field to be thrown in.

Breezy had almost forgotten about all of the other players. She turned around, rubbing the ball with both hands, glove under her arm. At least there was somebody standing at—or near—every position. But Jazz was watching the guys on the other team from her spot in rightfield, instead of concentrating on home plate. Julie was standing directly on top of second base. Betsy and Sarah were talking to each other in left-center. Breezy shook her head. She hoped she could strike everyone out and the Pink Parrots wouldn't have to show Tony's Pizzeria that they couldn't catch or throw to save their lives. At least Kim was leaning forward, knees bent, ready to get things going, and Crystal was trying to imitate Kim. And she was standing in exactly the right spot for a first baseman.

Suddenly, the stands erupted with shouts and cheers. Breezy turned back around to see the first batter, John Finnegan, step up to the plate. He took a few swings as he settled in his stance. "Come on, Finn!" came a shout from his dugout. "Let's get things going right away!"

Breezy took a deep breath and looked for Terry's signal. One finger hitting her leg twice. Fastball, inside. Breezy blew another bubble and went into her windup. Her fastball just nicked the inside corner of the plate, backing John off the plate a little. "Stee-rike!" the umpire shouted.

John glared at her, but Breezy didn't pay any attention. She had him off balance now. She delivered a change-up and another inside fastball for strikes two and three.

"Way to go, Breeze!" Kim shouted at her friend. "Keep it up!"

Ro yelped from the edge of the dugout. "All right, Breezy! Do it again!" she cheered, clapping her hands.

After Terry threw the ball back, Breezy was tempted to throw it around the infield to keep everyone in the game. But she was afraid that someone, or everyone— except Kim—would miss it. It wouldn't be good to let Tony's see all of their weak spots.

Greg Gromada stepped up to the plate. Tony's second batter went into his crouch slowly. Breezy waited until he had finished swinging the bat around. Terry called for a change-up. Breezy then threw the pitch right down the center for strike one. On the second pitch, a fastball, the batter got a piece of it and fouled off. Strike two.

"Come on, Greg!" Coach Manuli yelled from near first base. "Don't let a girl strike you out!"

Greg swung his bat furiously, and got set again. "One more!" Kim yelled. "You can do it!" Breezy glared at him before going into her windup. It never hurt to do a little intimidating, she figured. The ball whizzed in, clipping the outside corner of the plate for strike three.

"Way to go, Breeze!" Kim called. "One more out!"

"Yeah!" Crystal screamed, jumping up and then

crouching down again.

Breezy looked around the infield. Everyone seemed to be paying attention. She really hoped none of them touched the ball, though. And . . . Breezy squinted at rightfield, not believing what she saw. Jazz was doing *handstands* in the outfield! Breezy prayed not one hit went out to her cousin. The Pink Parrots would really be in trouble then.

"Come on, Julius!" the other team screamed as a tall black kid stepped up to the plate. Breezy remembered Pat Julius from last year. He would swing at almost anything, but unfortunately he almost always got a hit. Nobody had any idea how he did it. Pat pushed his glasses up and stared at Breezy, grinning.

"Groove it in!" Kim yelled at her. "You can strike him out!"

Breezy shook off Terry's first signal for a fastball. Pat would definitely get a piece of it. She took the change-up and delivered. Pat's bat blurred as he swung a little late, but he nicked the ball and it flew out toward shortstop. Breezy held her breath. Then she let it out after Kim caught it easily.

"O.K.!" Ro screamed, as Kim raced past Breezy toward the dugout.

"What are you waiting for, Breeze?" Kim asked, teasing her friend. "Let's get going!"

Ro patted Breezy on the shoulder when she jogged into the dugout. "One-two-three! Way to go!" Ro said.

But Breezy hardly even heard the congratulations. She was already thinking about batting. She was up first. She put on a batting helmet, picked up her bat and headed out to the plate.

"Let's go, Breezy!" Crystal screamed from the dugout. "Hit it!" Kim giggled behind her. Well, Crystal was sort of getting into it. Who knows, maybe she would become a good player after all, Breezy thought. Then she shook her head to clear her mind and concentrated on hitting. She stepped into the batter's box.

Pat was pitching. He wasn't as good as Joey Carpenter was, but he had a really sneaky change-up. Breezy decided she would watch for the fastball. Pat went into his windup and tried to whiz one right down the middle of the plate. Breezy quickly stepped over the plate and slipped the bat through her loose left hand. The ball hit the bat for a perfect bunt, and stopped only a few feet from home plate. Breezy didn't hesitate. She sprinted up the baseline to first. She beat the throw to John Finnegan by at least five seconds.

Resisting the impulse to smile, Breezy handed her batting glove to Ro. "All right!" Ro said, patting her on the back. "Nice bunt! You really caught them napping."

Breezy nodded. "Come on, C.J.!" Breezy yelled from first. The tall black girl stood with her knees locked too far forward in the batter's box. Crystal had told Breezy that she hadn't finished the section in her "how-to" book on batting yet. "Relax your knees and move back a little!"

Breezy yelled at Crystal.

Pat threw a pretty slow pitch right up the center of the plate. Crystal let it go by for strike one. "Keep your eye on the ball!" Kim called from near the backstop. She was swinging two bats around, trying to loosen her arms up. She was up next.

Crystal swung way too early on the next pitch. From first base, it looked to Breezy as if the ball had just left Pat's hand when Crystal whiffed. Breezy hoped her teammate would read the batting section soon.

Pat fired another strike and caught Crystal looking again. Poor C.J., Breezy thought, she didn't even try on that one. Walking away from home plate with her bat dragging and her head down, Crystal looked really disappointed. "Don't worry about it!" Ro called out from the coach's box next to first. "You'll get 'em next time!"

"Easy out!" Finnegan yelled from his spot next to Breezy at first base as Kim stepped up to bat. "The bat's bigger than she is!"

Breezy felt like hitting Finn. He could be so obnoxious sometimes. He and Pat Julius had been on the same team last year, too. Finn was an O.K. player, but he wasn't great. But then, she realized that he had never actually seen Kim hit before—Kim had been on the bench all last year! He was really in for something now, Breezy thought to herself.

Kim rapped the very first pitch into the hole between the second baseman and the centerfielder. Breezy slid into the base just a nanosecond before the ball got to the second baseman. So now the Parrots had a runner on first and second, and Terry was up.

Terry DiSunno was actually one of the most feared sluggers in Emblem—right after Peter Tolhurst. She had a ferocious swing and a mean temper that made her hit the ball even harder. But she was unpredictable and struck out a lot, too. That didn't stop pitchers from worrying, though, when they saw her step up to the plate. The longest blast Breezy had seen from Mitchell Lumber's bench last year had been Terry's, not Peter's. It had happened in the second-to-last game of the season and Terry had belted a grand-slam home run to win the game. What Breezy remembered about it was that Terry never even cracked a smile her entire way around the bases.

Terry let two strikes go by before swinging. The ball sailed over the leftfielder's head and bounced in the warning track. Breezy took off like a shot and flew around third base without even slowing down. She slid into home just as Pat got the cutoff throw at the mound. Dusting herself off, Breezy was surrounded by her teammates. Ro gave her a quick hard hug. "Way to hustle, Breezy!" Ro said. As she walked back to the dugout, Breezy turned and grinned at Terry, who was standing on second base. Terry actually smiled back at her.

Andrea and Julie both struck out one-two-three, leaving Kim and Terry stranded on base as the first inning ended. But when Breezy put her glove back on and headed out to the pitcher's mound, she couldn't help smiling a little. The Pink Parrots were leading! They were actually ahead in their first game!

The second and third innings passed pretty quickly. Breezy struck out the next six batters in a row. Unfortunately, the next six Pink Parrots struck out as well, including Breezy. In the top of the fourth inning, Sarah took over as pitcher and Breezy went out to centerfield. And that was when disaster struck.

Sarah wasn't a bad pitcher, but she didn't have the consistency that Breezy did. She couldn't stop people from getting hits. And hits were what Breezy had been afraid of. No one, except she and Kim, could field the ball, to say nothing of making the throw to first. Tony's Pizzeria had a field day in the fourth inning. They got eight hits and five runs before the Pink Parrots were able to retire the side. They added four more runs in the fifth inning and six more in the sixth. And to add insult to injury, the Pink Parrots didn't get *one* hit for the rest of the game. Breezy was furious! The Pink Parrots lost the game 15-1.

"What a blowout!" Breezy said after the game was over. She threw her bat into the dugout, followed immediately by her cap. Tony's Pizzeria was not that good. There was no way any decent team would have allowed 15 runs in just 3 innings, Breezy fumed. And to think that she had gotten only one hit all game! Her batting average was garbage. And she was exhausted from trying to cover the entire outfield, where she had moved when Sarah came in to pitch, by herself. If only they could have stopped after the first inning. . . .

10

"They really should have called that game due to extreme embarrassment!" Joey said loudly while Breezy was opening her locker on Monday morning. Breezy couldn't figure out what he was even doing near her locker. His own locker was two flights down and practically on the other side of the school.

"I heard it was really pitiful!" Joey's friend Sean agreed. Joey and some of his gang were leaning against the lockers across from Breezy's. Breezy clenched her fists and tried to remain calm. Those two were such jerks, she thought. She was *not* going to let them get to her.

"Maybe they'll get kicked back into T-ball," Joey continued, referring to the league for six and seven year olds. In T-ball they don't even have pitchers, just tees for the balls to rest on at home plate.

"Jerks!" Breezy hissed under her breath. She threw her jacket into her locker, missing the hook completely, and grabbed a couple of notebooks off the top shelf. She told herself not to turn around and scream at Joey.

The whole group of boys suddenly erupted in laughter. "Well, what do you expect?" Joey asked his friends. "They're just a bunch of girls! I can't wait until Mitchell Lumber plays them this Saturday."

Breezy slammed her locker shut. That was the last straw. She whirled around. She knew the Pink Parrots had been really bad on Saturday. In fact, they had been terrible. But that didn't give Joey the right to be so obnoxious.

"Don't lose your cool," Peter Tolhurst said, suddenly stepping in front of Breezy. He put a hand on her shoulder and then turned to Joey and his followers. "Shut your mouth, Carpenter!" he yelled across the hall. "Don't you guys have anything better to do?"

Joey looked shocked at Peter's outburst. Peter was well liked around school. He was known for his even temper and great sense of humor. And because he was such a good athlete, a lot of guys wanted to hang out with him. But he never hooked up with any particular group. He just floated around, fitting in with practically everyone—the jocks, the brains, even Lindsay's crowd.

Joey recovered quickly, though. "What? Is she your *girlfriend* now, Tolhurst?" he asked snidely.

Breezy could have killed Joey for saying that. She noticed that Peter's neck turned bright red. She could feel her own face burning as she stiffened and leaned away from Peter. She *was* going to kill Joey for saying that. She started to march toward Joey, but Peter stopped her.

"It's not worth it," Peter said quietly. "Come on, let's get out of here." He grabbed her arm and started walking. Breezy looked back and saw Joey grinning at them as Peter dragged her down the hall. Breezy couldn't help herself—she still wanted to hurt him somehow.

"Why'd you let him get away with that?" Breezy demanded as soon as they got to homeroom.

Peter smiled, his green eyes crinkling at the corners. "You never give up, do you?" he asked her, laughing.

Breezy sputtered. "What are you talking about?" she asked him, a little confused. "Joey was being a total jerk and you were letting him get away with it!" She dropped into her desk chair, slamming her books down.

Peter sat down at the desk in front of her. "Breezy, he just wants to be the center of attention. The more you yell back at him, the more you encourage him. If you would walk away, instead, he would just stop."

Now Breezy was really confused. And Peter was starting to sound like Crystal. "But you were the one who yelled at him. You wouldn't let me say anything!" she exclaimed.

"Well, he was making fun of you," he said, looking away from her. "I don't care what he says about me, but . . ." He stared at the floor.

Feeling flustered, Breezy didn't know how to respond. Did he think she was a wimp or something? Then why would he tell her that she never gave up? Peter was being really strange, she decided.

Peter cleared his throat and looked up again. "Anyway," he continued briskly, "I'm sorry you guys lost on Saturday. But you pitched a great game! How many strikeouts did you have?"

"Eight," Breezy answered shyly. "How do you know how I pitched?" she asked a little more boldly.

Peter cleared his throat, and Breezy noticed that his neck had started turning red again. "I . . . uh . . . I watched the first three innings before my game started."

"You were there?" Breezy asked in surprise. She hadn't seen him there.

"Yeah," Peter admitted sheepishly. "I looked at the wrong time on the schedule and had an hour or so to kill before my game started," he continued, hurriedly. Breezy thought it sounded as if he was making it up as he went along.

"Well, I'm glad you weren't there for the next three innings," Breezy said, glancing at him. "It was a total blowout. I couldn't believe it! They just rolled all over us. And there was nothing we could do."

The final bell rang for homeroom. "Don't feel bad," Peter said as he stood up. "It was only your first game. You guys will do better. I know you will." He grinned down at her. "I better get to my desk. Can I walk you to English later?"

Breezy nodded and watched him walk to the other side of the room. She couldn't figure out what was going on. But at least it took her mind off the total blowout on

Saturday. She had never been on a team as bad as the Pink Parrots before. Joey was right. They were pitiful. Breezy didn't even know if they could win in the T-ball league. But one thing was for sure, Breezy was going to make them get better—no matter what.

The week passed in kind of a blur for Breezy. She tried really hard to concentrate on school, but she kept thinking about the Pink Parrots. Ro had held two practices, on Tuesday and Thursday. And they had worked on skills both days for most of the time. Breezy couldn't believe it, but C.J. was actually starting to catch the ball with some regularity and Andrea and Julie could make the throw to first base two out of three times.

And now it was Friday night. Breezy and Kim were hanging out at the Hawks' house watching stupid horror movies when the phone rang. Breezy ran to pick it up.

"Hello," Breezy said into the phone.

"Breezy?" Crystal asked on the other end.

"Hey, C.J.!" Breezy greeted her enthusiastically. She plopped down in the big easy chair next to the phone. "What's up?"

"I'm sorry to bother you . . . ." Crystal began.

"Kim and I were just watching a movie. Don't worry about it," Breezy said.

"Well, I don't want to keep you from it," Crystal

continued a little apologetically.

"C.J., O.K. already!" Breezy exclaimed impatiently. She looked over at Kim and raised her eyebrow. Kim giggled. "What's up?" Breezy asked.

"Well, I was reading the chapter about bunting in my baseball book," Crystal said quietly. She paused, and Breezy had to bite her tongue from yelling at Crystal to spit it out. "And I was wondering when the best time to bunt is."

Breezy had to put her hand over her mouth to keep from laughing. Her shoulders were shaking and her eyes watered. On the sofa, Kim was giggling watching her best friend trying to hold it in. Breezy knew she couldn't look at Kim or she would really lose it. She took a deep breath and tried to think serious thoughts. Breezy couldn't believe how seriously C.J. took her baseball book. Because Breezy had played baseball for so long she couldn't imagine not knowing when to bunt. It was an instinct.

"Breezy?" C.J. asked uncertainly.

"It's hard to say," Breezy answered finally. "You never want to bunt when the other team is expecting it. The batter always wants to catch them napping, if you know what I mean. Sometimes, I like to lead off a game with a bunt, like I did last week. But it's great to use in a sacrifice situation."

"A sacrifice situation?" Crystal asked, confused.

"You know, when you want to get the runner on first

to second base, but you'll be out," Breezy explained.

"Oh," Crystal said. "Advance the runners at the cost of your own out?"

Breezy thought about that. There was something about the way C.J. said things sometimes. . . . "Right," she finally replied.

"Breezy!" Kim called from the couch. "Do you want me to pause the movie?"

"I'm sorry," Crystal apologized once more. "I didn't mean to take you away from your movie. I better go. Thanks for the information."

"No prob," Breezy replied. "Any other questions— call."

"Thanks," C.J. said. "I'll see you tomorrow."

"O.K., get a good night's sleep," Breezy responded and then grinned. "You're going to need it. We're going to kick Mitchell Lumber's butt all over the field tomorrow!"

"I certainly hope so. Bye."

"Bye," Breezy replied and hung up the phone. "She cracks me up," she said to Kim, walking back to the couch.

"What did she want?" Kim asked, stuffing a handful of popcorn in her mouth.

Breezy laughed. "She wanted to know when the best time to bunt was," she said. "I guess I'm really glad now she's reading those books. I think she's learning a lot."

"I can't believe we're actually playing Mitchell Lumber tomorrow," Kim said, changing the subject. She hit the pause button on the VCR remote control and turned to her friend. "Don't you feel a little weird about it? I mean, we were on that team all last year. . . ."

"No way!" Breezy cut her off. "I can't wait to play them. We're going to *win*!"

"Well, practice went really well this week," Kim agreed thoughtfully. "You know, I think Ro actually knows what she's doing. At first, I wasn't sure at all. Especially all that Groucho Walking and stuff. But now, I think she's going to be a good coach."

"I guess so," Breezy agreed slowly. "She's not bad."

Kim threw a pillow at her friend. "Come on, Breeze. You know she's a good coach. Admit it."

Breezy frowned. Kim was always trying to get Breezy to admit it when she was wrong. And she certainly had been wrong about Ro. Even though she was a hairdresser and wore really weird clothes, Ro knew baseball. In fact, she had started to teach Breezy how to throw a sidearm fastball on Thursday. Breezy was really psyched to try it out on Saturday against Mitchell Lumber. "All right," she confessed grudgingly. She grabbed the remote control out of Kim's hand and switched the movie back on. "Ro knows a lot about baseball."

"Breezy!" Kim practically yelled.

"O.K., O.K.," Breezy replied, grinning. She knew Kim wouldn't rest until Breezy admitted that she had been wrong. "Ro's a good coach."

Kim sat back on the couch with a smug smile. "I told you."

Breezy plopped down next to her friend. "Be quiet and watch the movie," she said. Breezy would never admit it to Kim, but she was a little worried about tomorrow's game. Mitchell Lumber was good this year, and the Pink Parrots had already shown that they were not. But they had to win, Breezy thought. She was going to do everything in her power to make sure they did.

11

"Come on, Breezy!" C.J. screamed from first base.

"Let's go!" Ro called from the dugout.

"Only one more!" Kim yelled from shortstop.

Breezy didn't hear any of them as she stood on the rubber, leaning forward a little, watching for Terry's signal. It was the top of the fifth inning and there were two outs. Mitchell Lumber was up 1-0, but the game wasn't over yet. Ro had decided to have Sarah pitch for the first three innings, and then have Breezy pitch the last three. Breezy thought that was a pretty good idea. At least she could try to contain any blowout at the end. But to everyone's surprise, it wasn't a blowout. The Pink Parrots didn't even have a hit yet, but at least the fielders were holding together.

Carl Haggarty, the first baseman, was up to bat and Breezy had two strikes on him. But he had fouled off the last four pitches. Breezy was getting a little impatient. She just wanted to get him out of there.

Terry pointed three fingers down. That was their new

signal for the sidearm fastball. Breezy hadn't thrown it yet, but Terry was right. It was time to unveil it. She took a step back from the rubber and went into her windup. The next thing she heard was the thump of the ball hitting Terry's glove.

"Stee-rike three!" the ump called loudly.

Breezy allowed herself one small smile and jogged back to the dugout. But she wiped the smile off her face as soon as she sat down. They had only one more inning left to get Mitchell Lumber's run back. The Parrots just had to do it!

"Top of the order! Top of the order!" Ro called as she walked up and down in front of the dugout.

Jumping up and pulling on her batting glove, Breezy picked up her favorite bat. She had forgotten that she was up. She hopped out of the dugout and went to stand next to the batter's box. Last night Breezy had been determined to win this game, but today she wanted to win even more.

Coach Carpenter had been totally obnoxious to Ro before the game. He kept calling her "little lady" and "doll." Breezy couldn't believe that Ro had kept her cool, but after Coach Carpenter walked back to his own dugout, Ro let loose with something about that "sexist, male chauvinist pig!" Then she said that she hated to see bald men try to pretend that they weren't. Coach Carpenter was completely bald on the top of his head, but he grew the hair on one side of his head longer than on the other side. Then he brushed all of the skinny strands over the top. Breezy and Kim had always laughed at him when a strong wind came along and made those long hairs stand straight up.

And then there was Joey. Joey had pitched an amazing first three innings. But he had been, as usual, a complete jerk about it. Breezy acknowledged that he was a very good pitcher, but she would never tell him that. He kept heckling her every time she came up to bat. Kim, too. And not *one* of the Pink Parrots could get a hit off him. It was almost too much for Breezy to handle.

Now Brian was pitching. Terry had popped up in the fourth inning, and the next five girls struck out through the fifth inning. But now Brian had to face the top of the order. Breezy was determined that she wouldn't go down without a fight.

"Batter up!" the umpire called.

"Come on, Breezy!" someone from her dugout yelled. "Let's get something going!"

Breezy took a deep breath and tried to ignore the shouts of "easy out" that were circulating around Mitchell's infield. She went into her crouch.

Brian's first pitch came right down the middle of the plate, and Breezy's bat caught a piece of it. She sent a line drive right between the first and second basemen out to leftfield. Breezy dropped the bat and sprinted up the first base line. She didn't even have to hear the ump's "Safe!" to know that she was.

Her teammates cheered and clapped. Ro ran over to congratulate her and take her batting glove. "Way to go," Ro said.

Breezy smiled at the coach briefly and got set for the next batter. She had to keep her mind on the game. C.J. was stepping up to the plate. She swung the bat a little nervously before settling into an awkward stance.

"Ea-sy out!" Carl screamed from first. "Her strike zone is so big that anything will be a K," he said, referring to the symbol used to mark a strikeout on a scorecard.

Breezy gritted her teeth to keep herself from saying anything. It wasn't worth it. C.J. would just have to show them. She held her breath as Brian went into his windup.

Crystal let the first three pitches go by without moving. Then with the count 2-1, she executed the most perfect bunt Breezy had ever seen. The ball barely traveled four feet away from the bat. And the infield was definitely caught napping.

Breezy scooted over to second base, but Crystal got thrown out at first. She definitely should have beaten that out, Breezy thought. C.J. had stood at the plate for too long. She was going to have to get a quicker takeoff. But what a bunt!

C.J. looked pretty pleased with herself as she jogged back to the dugout. She looked over her shoulder at Breezy, who grinned at her. C.J. smiled back. Breezy crouched down a little at second base and put her hands on her knees. Kim was up next, and Breezy hoped that she would keep the Parrots alive.

"Come on, Kim!" Breezy yelled from second base. Kim grinned and settled in next to the plate.

"No batter, no batter!" Joey yelled from centerfield. "Get her out, Brian!"

Breezy resisted the urge to turn around and scream something nasty at Joey. He sounded a little nervous. She guessed he hadn't expected anyone to get on base. And of course, they only had one run on the Parrots.

Kim took the second pitch and tapped it right over the third baseman's head. Breezy ran for third anyway, and slid into the bag right before the ball arrived.

"Safe!" the umpire yelled. It was really close.

Now the Parrots had a runner on first and third, there was one out and Terry was up. "Come on, DiSunno!" Breezy yelled as Terry stepped up to the plate. Terry swung the bat ferociously a few times and turned toward Brian with a scowl. He took off his cap nervously and wiped his forehead with his glove before settling back on the rubber. He took a deep breath and delivered.

Without any delay, Terry took the first pitch. She slammed the ball out to the warning track in rightfield. A major blast! Breezy ran home. A few seconds later, Kim came zipping across the plate. She must have really motored to make it from first, Breezy thought. She gave Kim a quick hug and then cheered for Terry, who made it to second.

"Way to go, Terry!" Breezy screamed. To her surprise,

Terry gave her a really big grin and flung a fist in the air. Terry must be more into the Parrots than Breezy had thought. She seemed really happy about that hit, and she had been playing the whole game with an intensity that almost matched Breezy's.

Andrea and Julie both struck out to retire the Parrots. But Breezy didn't care. The Parrots were winning by one run! Now all she had to do was hold them in the bottom of the sixth.

She grabbed her glove and jogged out to the pitcher's mound slowly. Throwing a few warmup pitches to Terry, Breezy tried to forget just how much she wanted to win this game. She knew she had to settle down and concentrate on the next nine pitches. If she was lucky, that was all it was going to take.

Ross Klein was up first. Breezy grooved the first two pitches in, nicking the outside corner both times. She caught Ross napping both times. But he got a piece of her third pitch, a change-up, and popped the ball up behind the plate. Breezy held her breath as Terry, with a speed that belied her size, jumped up, threw her mask off and ran back to make the catch right in front of the backstop. One out.

Breezy blew a big bubble and looked up to face the next batter. It was Joey. The moment she had been waiting for. She took a deep breath and blew another major bubble.

"Come on, Breeze!" Kim screamed behind her.

Three fingers. Breezy thought that was a great idea to start with the sidearm fastball. Breezy went into her windup and delivered a rocket right down the middle of the plate. Joey didn't even blink. "Stee-rike one!" the ump called.

Breezy had to use all of her willpower not to grin. She *was* going to strike Joey out. She knew it. Terry called for a change-up. Breezy delivered, but Joey caught a piece of it and popped it off into the stands.

"Stee-rike two!" the ump called.

Joey got a piece of Breezy's next *five* pitches. The sweat was dripping down the back of her neck now, and Breezy lifted her ponytail to get a little air. She was starting to feel the pressure now. She *had* to get that last strike. Terry called for an inside fastball.

Breezy went into her windup and threw the hardest pitch she had ever thrown. The ball whizzed by Joey before he had gotten the bat off his shoulder. He swung seconds too late. "Stee-rike 3!" the ump yelled.

Yelping in excitement, Breezy had to control the urge to jump up and down. The Pink Parrots were only one out away from winning their first game—and it was against Mitchell Lumber!

Butch Jacobs swaggered up to the plate and glared at Breezy. Breezy knew that glare from sitting on Mitchell Lumber's bench for so long. He was determined to get a hit. But she was as determined to get him out. She grooved the first pitch up the middle of the plate. Butch

115

swung and the ball blasted out toward rightfield.

"Oh, no!" Breezy exclaimed, turning around. Jazz was in rightfield. And she wasn't paying attention, as usual. In fact, it looked as if she was doing a back walkover or something, just as she had been during the last game. Breezy couldn't believe it! Her cousin was about to mess up again. What had ever made Breezy think that Jazz could play ball?

Jazz finished and stood up—facing the outfield wall. She thrust her arms up into the air like her gymnastics teacher had always taught her to do at the end of the routine. Her glove was open in just the right way and—*whap!*—the fly ball landed neatly in the pocket. Jazz was in shock, but instinctively she closed the glove around the ball and spun around.

Breezy had shut her eyes, but at the sound of Ro's wild cheering she opened them. She blinked three or four times, fast. She couldn't believe what she saw. Jazz was standing out in rightfield, holding her glove aloft—and the ball was in it. The Pink Parrots had actually done it! They had won! The air was filled with flying gloves as the whole team tossed them up in excitement.

After everyone calmed down a little, the entire Mitchell Lumber team reluctantly headed over to the Parrots for the mandatory congratulations. Breezy could tell they were pretty shocked that they had lost. The Parrots lined up and the players from the other team starting walking down the line, slapping hands and mumbling "Congratulations" and "Good game."

"Good going, Yardley," Kevin said to Kim, who was standing in line in front of Breezy. Kevin tugged on one of her braids. Breezy noticed the dirty look Joey gave Kevin, but Kevin didn't see it. "You guys played a gutsy game," he added.

Breezy just smiled at him as he walked by. She didn't think she'd ever stop smiling. Then Joey stepped in front of her. "You were just lucky," he mumbled, and then slapped her hand feebly. "We'll kill you next time!"

But Breezy knew that it was more than just luck. The Pink Parrots were getting to be pretty good. They had beaten Mitchell Lumber fair and square. "I can't wait!" Breezy shot back, and she meant it.

After Mitchell Lumber had been through the entire line, Ro called everyone over to the dugout. "Come on, guys!" she practically screamed. "We're going to celebrate! Let's go get ice cream at the Neptune Diner!"

The whole team shouted their agreement. After gathering up their equipment, they followed Ro the four blocks to the diner. Breezy felt as if a weight had been lifted off her shoulders. She was really proud to be the captain of the Pink Parrots.

"Who wants what?" Ro shouted above the din as they burst into the diner. "My treat!"

The Pink Parrots all shouted, "Yay!" and rushed to get two adjoining booths.

"I can't believe we won!" Kim exclaimed, her face still

117

flushed with excitement over the win.

"I knew we could do it!" Breezy replied.

"Right, Breeze," Kim said, feigning a look of shock. "You weren't worried one little bit, were you?"

"Nope," Breezy replied calmly. "C.J.," she said turning to Crystal, "That was one mean bunt. Picture perfect."

Crystal blushed and looked down. "Thanks, Breezy. That chapter was really helpful."

Breezy burst out laughing. "I might have to read that book after all."

"Parrots!" Ro called, standing up between the booths. "I just wanted to say that you girls did a great job today and I'm really proud of you. And . . ."

She paused, as the door opened. Marcel from the beauty salon walked in with a big box and put it down in front of Ro.

" . . . the uniforms are in," Ro concluded.

"All right!" Breezy exclaimed, jumping up to help Ro rip the box open. She had forgotten all about uniforms. Now, the Pink Parrots *really* were a team!

The box open, Breezy reached inside to grab a uniform. She pulled one out, suddenly yelped and dropped the jersey as if it had burned her. It was the same pink as their hats. Breezy couldn't believe it! A pink uniform? How could a baseball team be taken seriously if their jerseys were pink?

Ro passed out the uniforms, as Breezy sat down in

disbelief. Eddie started taking orders.

Breezy didn't even notice that he was barely even paying attention because he was so busy staring at Ro.

"I think Eddie likes Ro," Kim whispered to Breezy.

Breezy looked up and saw Eddie gaping at Ro with his mouth open, not even paying attention to anyone.

"Breezy!" a boy called from the back of the diner. Breezy whipped around in the booth and saw Peter Tolhurst waving at her. Kim giggled. "And I know *he* likes *you*!"

"Shut up, Kim!" Breezy ordered. "He probably just wants to congratulate us on winning." Why did Kim have to keep saying that Peter liked her? It was totally ridiculous, and if Kim didn't stop it she would kill her.

"Right," Kim said, smirking at Crystal. "We believe you, right C.J.?"

Crystal nodded, smiling. "Right," she agreed.

Breezy glowered at them both. "Well, aren't you going to go say hello to him?" Kim asked, practically pushing her friend out of the booth.

Breezy stood up and started walking back to Peter's table, where he was sitting with some of the guys from his team. She *was* going to kill Kim—later. But right now she felt too happy about the Pink Parrots' first win. And she had a funny feeling that it was only the beginning of an incredible season.

About the Authors

Kathilyn Solomon Proboz

Kathliyn lives in an old house in Cornwall, New York with her husband, her baseball glove, her piano and plenty of ghosts. She is going to take up rock climbing soon and is sure that girls can do anything boys can do and dares you to say otherwise. This is her first book.

Leah Jerome

Halfway to a Master's Degree in Education, Leah loves sports—especially baseball. She has followed the Mets since she was nine and likes to go to at least one home game a season. She lives in Ossining, New York. This is her second book.

Watch for

ALL THAT JAZZ

Number 2 in **The Pink Parrots** *series!*

"Come on Jazz, get with the program!" Ro said, "You're up." Ro cracked her gum and handed Jazz a batting helmet.

Jazz felt someone give her a little shove. She turned around. It was Breezy. "Give it all you've got, Jazz," her cousin said, pushing her out of the dugout. "This is our last chance."

It was the bottom of the sixth inning, there were two outs and Terry was on third base. And it was Jazz's turn at bat. Jazz had gotten on base exactly once before when she had been marched ... no, that wasn't right ... walked. She had been walked.

Jazz took a deep breath, stepped up to the plate and lifted the bat to her shoulder.

"Come on, Jazz!" called Terry from second. "Just get on base! Keep us alive!"

That was easy for Terry to say—she had gotten plenty of hits. But Jazz was the strikeout queen of the Pink Parrots.

"Hey, Jazz!" Ro yelled from the bench. "You're standing too close to the plate. Try to back up a little!"

"Jazz!" Terry called out. "Your hands are reversed! Put the right one on top!"

Jazz switched her hands and took a deep breath. She squeezed her eyes shut for a moment and wished as hard as she could that she would hit the ball. Jazz opened her eyes again. She knew she was supposed to concentrate and look at the pitcher, but all she could think about was how cute he was. Jazz definitely did not want him to see her like this—all wet and disgusting.

The first pitch whizzed by her. Jazz didn't even see it. She heard it hit the catcher's mitt and then the umpire yelled, "Strike one!"

Jazz squinted her blue eyes in concentration. She was really going to try and get a hit. The pitcher grinned at her and then went into his windup. As soon as she saw the ball, Jazz swung.

To her surprise, the bat vibrated as it made contact with the ball. Jazz just stood and watched as the ball flew over the head of the shortstop and bounced in front of the leftfielder. She couldn't believe it. She had hit the ball! She had actually hit the ball! Suddenly, she thought baseball was absolutely the greatest thing in the whole world!